TERROR IN THE SNOW!

Dad and Grampa just stood there and looked. After a minute or so, Grampa walked over to where the dead calf was. Real slow, he knelt down and looked at something in the snow. It was a track of some kind. He traced around it with his finger, frowning, like he usually did when he was trying hard to remember something.

Then, like lightning, he was on his feet again, moving toward Dad and Tom.

"Hurry," he yelled, "get to the truck!"

Puzzled, they stared at him.

"Get to the truck! *Now!*"

There wasn't much that scared Tom's grandfather. The fact was, Tom had never known the old man to be afraid of anything. But when Grampa called out the second time, Tom heard the terror in his voice and knew that something had scared his Grampa—bad.

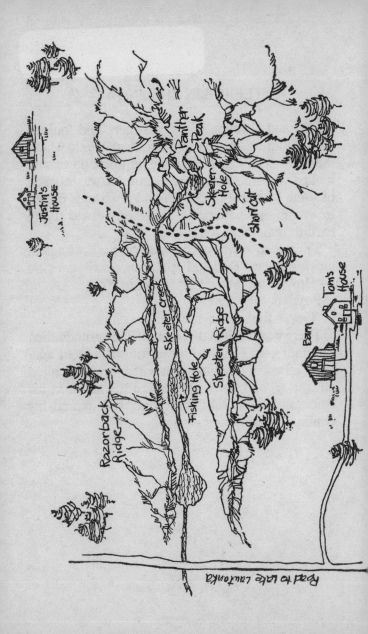

BILL WALLACE

DANGER ON PANTHER PEAK

(original title: *Shadow on the Snow*)

A MINSTREL™ BOOK

PUBLISHED BY
SIMON & SCHUSTER, INC.

This book is dedicated to Gary Gardner, for teaching me how to hunt and fish and find tracks that a big cat left in the sand near Skeeter Hole; and to the boys and girls in my fourth-grade homeroom, who told me the stories were good and who encouraged me to keep writing.

Originally published in hardcover by Holiday House under the title *Shadow on the Snow*.

 A MINSTREL BOOK, published by
Simon & Schuster, Inc., 1230 Avenue
of the Americas, New York, New York 10020

ISBN: 0-671-64116-6

First Minstrel Books printing January, 1987

First special printing December, 1986

10 9 8 7 6 5 4 3 2 1

A MINSTREL BOOK and colophon are trademarks of
Simon & Schuster, Inc.

Printed in the U.S.A.

DANGER
ON
PANTHER
PEAK

1

A big, brown rope hung just inside the front door of the barn, right where Tom had left it. With Dad and Grampa busy in the corral, and Mama and Susan busy in the house, there was no one left to watch him and yell, "Get down off that rope before you break your neck."

So he got the rope and wrapped it around his hand. He backed up to the stack of alfalfa and started to climb. About halfway up, he stopped, grabbed the rope with both hands, and took a flying leap.

For a split second, he was falling. The rope tightened in his hands, stopping his fall. It sent him in a swooping glide—down—then up again, sailing like the wind.

He swooped far out over the barnyard. The ground swirled past beneath him. Then he was facing the bright blue of the sky, and again, falling backward, toward the barn. The wind stirred his hair and made the breath of hot summer seem almost cool on his neck.

There was a sudden darkness as the swing of the rope carried him back into the barn. Then, once more, he swooped into the bright summer day. Then back again into the barn. In and out—back and forth— until the rope slowed its swing.

Tom slid to the ground, carefully, so the rope wouldn't burn his hands. Then, grabbing the big knot at the end, he climbed back to his perch on the haystack and got ready to swing again.

He had just reached the right bale when the sound of his father's voice stopped him.

Tom stayed as quiet as he could. He pressed himself back against the hay so he wouldn't be noticed.

His father and grandfather looked small from up where he was. His father was bigger than Grampa Burke. His legs carried him faster and his back was straighter. Grampa had a funny way of waddling when he walked—not like a duck, but much brisker. And his feet shuffled back and forth, real quick-like. His shoulders were a little stooped, sort of bent over with his age. Still, he didn't seem to have much trouble keeping pace with Dad as they moved across the barn-yard.

Tom watched them until they disappeared around the side of the barn and headed out to where the hay truck was parked. When they were gone, he took a good hold of the rope and leaped off the haystack.

Back and forth he swung, way out over the barnyard, then in and out of the doorway, quick as a wink. He was free as an eagle without a care in the world.

"Tom Burke! You get down from there!"

The sudden shout startled him. The rope slipped through his hands, but he caught it, stopping his fall. He looked down.

The ground was moving by so fast, it was hard to see. And when he turned his head, the rope started spinning. He was sailing back and forth—spinning round and round—both at the same time. Still, he managed to catch a quick glimpse of someone on the ground below him.

Then he sailed into the barn. Still whirling around, he came back out again, and saw a bright blue dress.

On the next swing, he saw red hair and a ponytail.

And as he started slowing down, he could see his sister's freckled face glaring up at him.

"You get down off there, right now," she threatened. "You get down or I'll tell Mama."

"I ain't hurting nothing," Tom yelled as he swung back into the barn. "Why don't you . . ."

He finished the sentence when he swung back out.

". . . leave me alone."

"Mama told you not to play up there," Susan scolded.

"Go away."

"Not till you get off that rope."

"No."

"I'll tell Mama."

The rope had almost stopped swinging. Tom glared at his big sister. He stuck out his tongue.

"Tattletale."

Susan put her hands on her hips.

"I'm gonna tell Mama. She said she'd get you next time you stuck your tongue out at somebody. I'm gonna tell."

She kicked up some dust as she spun around and started walking real fast, toward the house.

It didn't take much to figure out what she was going to do.

Tom stuck out his tongue again, and started singing:

"Tattletale, tattletale. Sittin' on a bull's tail . . ."

Susan hesitated, like she was going to stop and argue with him some more, but instead, she started running.

Tom clung to the rope until Susan went between the two big cedar trees at the front edge of the yard. Then he dropped, hitting the ground at a dead run. He reached the cedar trees just as Susan opened the front door. She went in, yelling for Mama, and as soon as the screen door bounced shut behind her, Tom took out for the back of the house.

He snuck under the kitchen window, and when he got to the edge of the door, he froze in his tracks. He held his breath and listened.

"All right. All right..." he could hear Mama's voice moving toward the front part of the house. "... I'll go talk to him. I just wish you two would quit fussin' with each other. Beats me how you can love on each other and be sweet one minute, then be fighting like cats and dogs the next..." She kept muttering and mumbling clear through the house.

Just as soon as Tom heard the front screen bounce shut, he opened the back door and went in. He closed it real quiet, so nobody could hear, then tiptoed through the kitchen and went up the stairs.

He needed a good place to hide out until things cooled down.

"Grampa's room is my best bet," Tom decided. After closing the door behind him he lay down on the floor on the far side of Grampa's bed.

He stared up at the ceiling for a long while. He stayed real still. Then he heard Mama's voice calling his name. It grew louder as she moved from the barn and headed back toward the house. He held his breath for a moment, trying as hard as he could to be quiet, but the louder her voice got, the more he started to wiggle and fidget. Finally, he rolled over on his side.

There, right in front of his nose, was a huge shotgun. Tom had never seen Grampa's shotgun before—'course, he'd never looked under Grampa's bed before either.

Tom felt his eyes scrunch up a little as he strained to see in the darkness.

The old gun was a ten-gauge, double-barrel. Tom remembered that from hearing Grampa talk about it. The long barrels were kind of brown and rough from the layers of rust that had built up. There were two big hammers with swirls and designs etched into the steel. On the side of the gun, there was a picture of buffalo carved into the plate. Tom took hold of the thick wood stock and turned it over. The thing was so big and heavy, he had to struggle with it. On the other side there was a picture of a deer and a mountain lion. Even with the rust, he could see the pictures. It was a beautiful old gun.

He had to get up on his knees and use both hands to drag it out from under the bed. The shotgun was heavy as could be, but just holding it made him feel big and strong, like the cowboys used to be.

"You're *really* gonna get it now!"

Tom almost jumped out of his skin at the sound of

his sister's voice. He'd been so busy looking at Grampa's shotgun, he hadn't heard Susan open the bedroom door and come sneaking in. He almost dropped the gun, but caught it and looked up. Susan was just a few feet away. She had her hands on her hips and that snotty big-sister sneer on her face.

"Mama finds out you been playing with Grampa's gun, she'll . . . well, she'll ground you for the rest of your life."

Tom didn't argue with her. Instead, he got up and lay the gun on the bed.

"You see this?" he asked, leaning over and looking at it.

"What?" Susan growled.

"The pictures and stuff carved into the side of this thing."

She moved a step or two closer. Tom glanced over his shoulder at her.

"Isn't it pretty? Look how clear it is and all the little lines—like you can see the hair on the buffalo's chin."

She was standing right beside him now, admiring the fine artwork. He turned it over and showed her the picture of the deer and the mountain lion.

Susan was quiet for a moment. Then: "Mama says you're never to play with guns and if she—"

"I wasn't playing with it." Tom kept his voice soft.

"I was hiding in here and I saw it under the bed. I was just looking at it."

Susan sighed. "It *is* beautiful. Now, you put it up 'fore Mama catches you."

"You gonna tell her about the gun?"

Susan scrunched her mouth up on one side and shrugged.

"No. But you hurry up and get downstairs. She's mad 'cause you hid from her."

Tom felt a sigh of relief whoosh out of his chest when he put the gun back under the bed.

Sometimes, having a big sister wasn't all that bad. Then again . . .

2

Tom was grounded for a day, but at least Susan hadn't said a thing to Mama about him playing with Grampa's gun. The minute they had gotten downstairs, Susan had griped and fussed about how Tom was always sticking his tongue out and calling her names. Then she'd reminded Mama about how he'd run off and hid from her.

Being grounded hadn't been so bad. In fact, Tom really couldn't tell the difference between being grounded yesterday and not being grounded today.

"When you're grounded, you *can't* do anything. And when you're not grounded, there isn't anything to do anyway. So, what's the difference?" he said out loud as he sat alone on the top step of the front porch.

"What are you saying?"

The sound of Grampa's voice startled Tom. He jumped and almost fell off the step. Grampa let the screen door bounce shut behind him and sat down beside Tom.

"When I came out the door, you were saying something."

Tom shrugged. "Oh, I was just talking to myself. That's all."

Grampa took his tobacco pouch out of his pocket and started filling his pipe.

"Sounds serious."

Tom frowned. "What does?"

"You talking to yourself. People usually got a pretty big problem on their mind when they take up talking to themselves."

Tom sighed. "Oh, it's not much, really. . . . It's just . . . well . . . yesterday, Mama grounded me for sassing Susan and sticking my tongue out. Today, I'm not grounded, but it don't make much difference. There's just nothing to do around here.

"Shoot, back in Enid, there was lots of stuff to do. I had a whole bunch of friends: Jason, Chris, and Luke. We'd get together to play football or ride our bikes or go to the show—anytime we wanted. Since we moved here, well, there's not even anybody around for miles. We're way out here in the sticks."

Grampa scrunched his tobacco down in his pipe with a wrinkled finger.

"Tom, you only been here a couple of weeks. Ever think about getting out and finding something to do?"

"There ain't nothing to do."

"Have you looked?"

Tom snorted. "Looked far enough to find the rope in the barn, but that only got me in trouble with Susan and Mama."

"Well, there's lots of other stuff."

Tom shook his head. "No. Think I'll just sit here."

They sat quietly, for a long time. The only sound was the squeak from the old wood step that came when either of them would shift his weight. Finally, Grampa nudged Tom with an elbow.

"You know, Tom, in the two weeks since you moved here, the farthest I've seen you away from the house is the corner of the barnyard. Now, when I was your age, I used to do a powerful lot of exploring. See them hills yonder?"

He pointed with the end of his pipe. There was a ridge about a half mile to the east—a place where it looked like some big rocks popped out of the ground. Just big rocks, and not much more.

"Yes, sir. I see it."

"Well, they don't look like much from here." Grampa struck a match on the seat of his overalls and lit his pipe. "But you get over close to 'em and they're regular mountains. I bet there's places over there that people ain't never set eyes on before. Probably caves, and canyons and gullies. Wouldn't be a bit surprised if there might not even be a waterfall or a hidden lake somewhere in them hills."

Tom was on his feet.

"Really? You think there's places that no one has ever seen?"

"You don't have to believe me, boy, if you don't want to." Grampa smiled. "Besides, you don't know nothing about exploring. You'd probably end up getting yourself lost, anyway."

Grampa stood up. Just before he went inside, he looked over his shoulder and made a growling sound with his throat.

"One thing. *If* you do decide to go exploring, you stay off Panther Peak."

"Huh?"

"Panther Peak," Grampa repeated. He pointed with the end of his pipe. "There's two ridges over there. Lot bigger and more rugged than they look from here. The one closest to us is called Skeeter Ridge; the far one is Razorback. Between the two is a valley with a little dab of water called Skeeter Creek. About three-quarters of a mile up the valley is a big, straight-up, smooth-faced ridge that leads to the top of that peak, yonder."

In the distance, Tom could make out the peak. It looked more like a tower rising up, with all but the flat, tree-covered top hidden by Skeeter Ridge.

"What's so special about that?" Tom asked. "It doesn't look much bigger or steeper than the other stuff around it."

Grampa took the pipe out of his mouth. "It ain't the climbing I'm worried about." He came back to where Tom was sitting on the step. "How do you suppose that place got its name? Not from bobcats or mountain lions. They call it Panther Peak because of the panthers—that's how it come by the name. Real, honest-to-goodness panthers. Some mighty big ones, too." He stuck the pipe back in his mouth and sat down. "My father used to tell me that in the winter of 1901, some hunters and trappers come in with fifty-seven pelts—all of 'em taken from around and on top of that one peak."

Tom hung his foot over the edge of the step and traced a circle in the dust.

"Grampa, 1901 was a long, long time ago. Except for zoos and stuff, there aren't any bears or mountain lions or wolves around here anymore. My teachers said so."

Grampa usually puffed his pipe slow and easy. Right now, it reminded Tom of a smokestack on some big factory.

"That's what I thought back in 1933. Figured the hunters had them all killed off and there were too many people around these parts for a big cat to want to stay within miles.

"But I was out hunting with my twenty-two one day when I stumbled right onto one. He come at me, and would have got me, too, if it weren't for an old hound I had named Slim. Old Slim weren't no match for that big gray cat, but he tore into him anyhow. Slowed him long enough for me to skin down that rock cliff and get to my horse."

Tom heard the step squeak when he leaned toward Grampa.

"Did it kill your dog?"

"Nope." Grampa smiled. "Old Slim was pretty scratched up and bleeding a lot, but he still managed to beat me and my pony back to the house."

It made for a good story, Tom thought, but he really didn't know if he believed Grampa or not. Even if it was true, 1933 was still way back in "the old days." He sighed and leaned back against the porch.

"You're just funnin' me, aren't you, Grampa?"

Only, Grampa wasn't smiling. His chin stuck out, strong and sharp.

"I ain't funnin' you, Tom. Not one bit! I don't know what it is, nor why, but ever so often—'bout ever' ten years or so—somebody driving through the Wichitas late at night will report seeing a big cat, or some farmer in the area will find some of his stock torn and half eaten.

"What makes 'em come, or how they manage to get here through all the people and highways and everything else, I flat don't know. But I do know what I'm telling you is *true*. And if you head out around those mountains, you stay clear of Panther Peak."

Grampa sounded sincere, Tom thought. But still . . .

"I'll probably just sit around here in the shade," Tom said. "Maybe there'll be something good on TV after awhile."

Grampa stood there beside him for a moment, then headed for the door. He made that growling sound again.

"You go ahead and sit there. Not that I can see what's so much fun about collectin' splinters off that old step. But if you like collectin' splinters in your rump, just go on sittin'."

The screen door bounced shut with a thud. As soon as Tom was sure his grandfather was gone, he jumped up and dusted his seat off. He felt around in his pockets, just to make certain there weren't really any splinters.

He looked toward the ridge of rock. "I bet they're just a pile of boulders," he thought with a frown. "I bet they aren't even mountains at all."

He scratched his chin. "But maybe there are mountains over there," he argued with himself. "I bet it would just take a few minutes to find out, and I bet I wouldn't get lost, either."

3

It was a lot farther than Tom thought. And it took him more than a half hour of walking just to reach the base of the first ridge, the one Grampa called Skeeter.

It *was* bigger than it looked from the house. The slope at the bottom was smooth and covered with small trees. Big round boulders—brownish-red with flecks of black mixed in—seemed to pop up everywhere. Beyond the first slope Tom could see a second, and beyond that, a third that climbed toward the tall and rocky ridge at the top.

Taking a deep breath, Tom started to climb. Blackjack trees sprang from large cracks between the boulders. He made his way around them, using the rough branches as handholds to help pull himself up over the smooth rocks.

It was more like walking up hill than climbing a mountain. He kicked at a little cactus.

I knew Grampa was just funnin' me, he thought. "This isn't a mountain at all. It's just slopes. Just little ole slopes."

After about twenty minutes, he came to the rockiest part of the ridge. A huge stone peak loomed before him. Jagged, sheer cliffs seemed to rise straight up into the sky. Giant round boulders cluttered the ground.

Tom smiled. "Now, that's a mountain," he told himself. "I wonder if this is Skeeter Ridge or Panther Peak? Up close, everything looks so different . . ."

He started to climb. About halfway up, Tom stopped. Clinging to the rocks, he looked back to see how far he had come.

Between him and the bottom of the ridge, there was only empty air. He suddenly realized that if he slipped, there was nothing to keep him from falling, clear to the bottom.

His breath stopped in his throat. He felt his hands shake. Frightened, he clung to the edge of the cliff. He pressed himself into it, as tight as he could.

For a long time, he was afraid to look around, afraid to move. But finally, he started climbing again. He tested each handhold in the cracks of rocks and made sure he had his feet planted firmly under him before he moved.

The climbing was hand over hand. Inch at a time, he pulled, strained, and squeezed his way through cracks and crevices between the huge stone boulders.

Finally, Tom reached the top. He was panting so hard he could barely hear the wind as it stirred the trees. On top of the ridge, the cedars looked strange. Their branches were twisted and gnarled. Instead of being thick and green, they were beaten and misshapen by the wind. They seemed old, older than anything he'd ever seen.

Still panting, he sat down under one of the trees and tried to catch his breath.

"One thing for sure," he thought. "I ain't going back down the face of that cliff. I'll find another way down from here—even if it takes all day. Climbing that cliff was the scariest thing I've ever done."

"You're kinda dumb, ain't you?" a voice said.

Tom jumped and looked around. The voice scared him. He was sure he was the only living thing on top of this ridge. But the voice had to come from some place. He twisted and looked in the other direction.

A boy was standing just a little ways behind the cedar tree he was sitting under. Tom got to his feet.

"What did you say?" he asked.

"I said you're kinda dumb. Only a dummy would come straight up Skeeter Ridge."

The boy stood with his hands in his pockets, smiling. He was about the same size and age as Tom.

"Who are you?" Tom asked.

The boy stuck his nose up in the air.

"Maybe it ain't none of your business," he snapped. "What's your name?"

Tom stuck his nose in the air, too. "Maybe it ain't none of *your* business."

The boy put his hands on his hips and glared at Tom. Tom put his hands on his hips and glared at the boy. The boy started walking around, sideways, looking Tom over. Tom moved in the opposite direction, looking the boy over.

"Only a dummy would climb up the cliff," the boy repeated.

"I came up that way 'cause I wanted to," Tom snapped. "I came up here to climb mountains, and that looked like the hardest way up."

The boy laughed. "You think you're a mountain climber, huh?"

Tom stepped right up to him and glared at him, eye to eye.

"That's right. You want to make somethin' of it?"

The boy stopped laughing. "I could if I wanted to," he said.

"Sure you could," Tom dared. "Like what?"

"Like beatin' you up."

"You and who else?"

"Don't need nobody else. I could whip you with both hands tied behind my back."

Tom laughed. "You talk a good fight. Why don't you do something?"

"I just might."

"Well, go ahead."

The boy set his feet. With both hands, he pushed Tom's shoulders. Tom braced himself and pushed the boy back.

"Dare you to do that again," the boy said.

Tom pushed him again.

"There," he boasted. "What are you gonna do about it?"

The boy pushed Tom.

They kept pushing each other back and forth. But that only lasted for a minute. They backed off, scrunched down, then pounced. . . .

They tore into each other like a couple of bulldogs scrapping over a bone. Slugging and hitting, wrestling, clinging together, they tumbled over and over. Dust whirled up around them so thick they could hardly see.

All of a sudden, Tom found himself on the bottom of the pile. The boy put both knees on Tom's shoulders. Then he started pounding him in the face with his fists.

It hurt something terrible. Tom rolled his head from side to side, trying to keep from getting hit.

"Holler uncle," the boy yelled. "Holler uncle and I'll let you go."

Tom struggled to get up. The boy was too heavy.

He rolled his head. The boy hit him in the ear.

He rolled his head the other direction.

His cheek brushed against the boy's leg.

All of a sudden, Tom opened his mouth, wrapping his teeth around the boy's leg. He bit down as hard as he could bite.

The boy yelled and jumped. Then Tom pushed up with all his might. It shoved the boy off balance. Tom scooted out from under him, and away they went again, tumbling and rolling down the hill.

How long they were at it, neither one of them knew for sure. They kept biting and scratching, yelling and hitting and fighting. Then, about halfway down the hill, they rolled smack into a big boulder. Hit it so hard, it knocked the wind out of both of them, throwing them apart.

They ended up on their hands and knees, facing one another. Their clothes were torn, and they had scratches and bruises all over them. Both were panting, and they could barely stand on all fours.

"You had enough?" the boy panted.

Tom took a deep breath. "You had enough?"

They waited a second, listening to each other breathe.

"Not unless you had enough," the boy puffed.

"I'm ready to go whenever you are," Tom bragged.

Then he got to thinking about what he'd said. Tired as he was, he didn't know if there was any more fight left in him.

Very slowly, both boys got to their feet, still glaring at each other. They were braced, ready to pounce.

"If you've had enough," the boy said, "I've had enough."

"Well," Tom said, "If you've had enough, I've had enough."

It was getting pretty late, judging by the way the sun was resting just on the top of the rock hills. Tom dusted the front of his jeans off. "Boy, am I gonna catch it when I get home," he said. "Guess I better go."

The boy nodded. "Me, too."

They had only gone a few steps in opposite directions when they both stopped and turned back to each other.

"You gonna be here tomorrow?" the boy asked.

"I guess. You?"

"I guess."

They looked at one another a second, then turned and started off. Suddenly, Tom remembered.

"Hey," he called. "What's your name, anyway?"

The boy smiled. "My name's Justin. Justin Harris. What's yours?"

"Tom Burke."

Justin waved.

"I'll see you tomorrow, Tom Burke."

Tom waved back.

"See you, Justin."

Mama was convinced that Tom had fallen off the mountain. She fussed and fretted while trying to clean him up. She kept saying how he shouldn't be playing up on those mountains, that they were dangerous.

All the time, Tom kept trying to tell her he hadn't fallen. But she wouldn't listen.

When she finally did start listening and understood that he got in a fight instead of falling off the hill, it was even worse.

"A fight?" Mama bit her lips and looked real worried. "I ought to ground you for the rest of the summer. I ought to . . . to . . . You get up to your room and clean *yourself* up. You'll go to bed without supper tonight. I reckon that's punishment enough."

"Yes, ma'am," Tom said as he scurried off toward his room.

He sat down on the edge of his bed. "Sure got off lucky this time," he thought out loud. "Guess Mama's feelin' sorry for me 'cause I've been sort of lonesome."

He went to the bathroom to wash up, then slipped into his pajamas. It was a warm night, so he didn't need any covers. A cool breeze came from the west. It made the curtains at the foot of the bed flip and flop.

Tom gazed up at the ceiling. The strands of moonlight that filtered through the trees outside his room cast strange shadows. In places, he could see mountains and valleys. And when the light moved just right, he could even imagine waterfalls and shimmering lakes.

"Wonder what time Justin will be there in the morning?"

He didn't know why he was thinking about Justin. It wasn't like he was a friend or anything. All the friends he had back home hardly ever fought.

But a smile came to his face. He almost laughed to himself. It was a pretty good fight, he remembered with a giggle.

"Maybe tomorrow," he thought, "if we aren't too busy fighting, we can find something else to do. Maybe explore together. Maybe go mountain climbing, or maybe . . ."

Before Tom knew it, the darkness of sleep had swallowed him. He slept until the first light of a new day.

4

Mama was still sore at Tom when he came down for breakfast the next morning. He could tell by the way she flipped and stomped around the kitchen, and by the fact she wouldn't talk to him.

After they finished eating and he got through helping Susan with the dishes, Dad motioned him out to the porch.

"Your Mom and I had a talk last night," he said. "I don't hold with your fighting either, but I can understand how it happened. You can go back and play with Justin. Just don't get in anymore fights. You do, Mama's going to be mad at both of us." He smiled and punched Tom on the shoulder. "I don't mind her being mad at you, but I sure don't want her mad at me."

At the bottom of the ridge, where Tom had met Justin, he went up an easier way. He walked around to the side of the first cliff and found a smooth path that led to the top.

From the crest of Skeeter Ridge, he could see his house. It seemed a long ways off. He turned and looked the other direction.

He could see the valley that Grampa had told him about, and the little creek that flowed through it.

The valley was only about a quarter of a mile wide. Beyond it, another ridge rose up sharp. It must be the second ridge Grampa had mentioned. It was a little higher than the one where he was standing.

He brought his eyes back to the valley, far below. He followed the stream as it twisted and jogged around the granite boulders and through the flats. It ended at the base of a big mountain. He studied it a moment, wondering where the stream had gone, then let his eyes take in the mountain.

Near the bottom, it was cluttered with huge boulders and trees. It seemed to rise up, slowly at first, then steeper and steeper. Finally, near the top, it shot straight up into a circle of smooth walled cliffs. Almost like a tower, crowned with trees, looming up high above the two ridges on either side.

"That's it," Tom whispered to himself. "That's Panther Peak."

"What is?"

The sound of Justin's voice startled him. Tom almost jumped clean out of his shoes. He wheeled around.

"How come you always sneak up on people?"

"I didn't sneak, I just walked up here." He squinted at Tom a minute. "You want to fight some more?"

Tom shrugged. "If you do."

Justin sat down on a big rock.

"I guess not. I got in trouble yesterday for tearing my clothes. If I do it again today, my mom's liable to kill me. You get in trouble?"

Tom shook his head.

"Not much. I just got yelled at and sent off to bed without supper. I'll probably get more than a talkin' to if I do it again, though."

He sat down on a rock close to where Justin was. Justin looked at him a minute, then frowned.

"You talking to yourself when I came up?"

Tom shrugged. He pointed to the huge, towering ridge at the far end of the valley. "I was just trying to figure out if that was the mountain that Grampa calls Panther Peak."

Justin nodded. "That's the one, all right. The old-timers around here got all sorts of neat stories about it. I figure most of it is just made up, though."

Tom smiled. "Yeah. Me, too."

He sat quiet for a minute, looking at the ridge. Then he asked, "Whereabouts is your house?"

Justin pointed over his shoulder with a thumb. "Other side of that ridge. Razorback Ridge, it's called. You can't see my house from here."

"Is it a long ways off?"

Justin looked at him. There was a mischievous twinkle in his eye.

"It would be if I was dumb enough to climb Razorback Ridge like you been climbing this one. Only, I know the shortcut. You want me to show you? You can see my house from there, too."

"Sure."

They got up and followed the ridge where they'd been sitting and headed toward Panther Peak. From Grampa's house, it looked like the two ridges ran right up against the towering peak. But when they were almost to the end of Skeeter Ridge, the ground sloped away into a wide, tree-covered canyon. Across the valley, it did the same between Razorback Ridge and the peak. The canyon was almost like a moat circling some ancient castle—like you'd see in a movie—only there wasn't any water there, just trees. It separated

Panther Peak from the two ridges.

"What's that called?" Tom wondered aloud.

Justin shrugged. "Don't reckon it's got a name. Just some old canyon."

Tom looked past where Justin was standing. There, in the hazy distance, stood a farmhouse with a barn and corrals.

"That yours?"

Justin looked over his shoulder. "Yep." He pointed behind Tom. "That your house?"

"Not really," Tom answered. "It's Grampa's. But we moved in a couple of weeks ago. Grandmother died about two years back, so Grampa asked Dad to come live with him and help take care of the place."

"Where did you used to live?" Justin asked.

"We lived in Enid. It's about a hundred fifty miles north of here."

"You ever live in the country before?"

"No," Tom said.

Justin shook his head. "Guess you don't know much about hunting and fishing and things like that."

Tom shrugged. "Guess not."

Justin seemed to brighten. "You like to learn?"

"Sure." Tom felt his eyes get real big. "How?"

"I reckon I could teach you." Justin pointed to the creek that ran between the two ridges. "That creek ain't very big, but there's a couple of good fishin' holes. 'Bout all's in there is perch—but they're a lot of fun to catch. You got a fishin' pole?"

Tom slumped back against a rock. "No."

"That's okay." Justin grabbed his hand and pulled him up. "I know how to make one. They work better than a store-bought thing anyhow. Come on."

They made their way down Skeeter Ridge—on the side where Justin's house was. Staying along the edge, they walked the flat ground until they came to a place where the creek widened into a round, deep pool.

The water was a dark green color. And being down low in the middle of all the trees, the wind could hardly reach it. Its surface was smooth as a mirror.

Justin walked over to a big tree and reached into a hole in its trunk. He pulled out a ball of twine, then reached in again and got a fishing cork with six or seven hooks stuck in it.

"Where did that stuff come from?" Tom asked.

Justin smiled. "I hid it here. There's about six fishin' holes along this creek. I got my tackle hid near each one of 'em. Saves me from having to carry all the stuff around."

Tom stood watching with his mouth open. It took Justin only a minute to find a long limb. He broke it from the tree and stripped all the leaves off it. Then he tied the string to one end and put the hook at the end of the string.

"Willow limb," he announced as he handed it to Tom. "Best fishin' pole ever made."

He broke off another and rigged up the same thing for himself.

"All set. All we got to do now is get the bait."

Tom was expecting Justin to go to another hiding place and pull out one of those plastic containers filled with worms, like he'd seen for sale in stores. Instead, Justin went up in the bushes. He started pouncing on grasshoppers and turning over logs and snatching up crickets.

When they went back to the edge of the water, he put one of the grasshoppers on Tom's hook and motioned for him to put his line in the water.

Tom did, and the grasshopper started kicking and splashing around on the surface. "Go on and let him sink," Justin whispered.

Tom lowered his pole some. When he did, the grasshopper went under. In just a second, he saw the tip of his pole bend. He watched it, holding his breath.

"You got one," Justin yelled.

Tom looked up at him.

"What do I do?"

"Yank on it, dummy!"

Tom yanked the pole toward him.

"No," Justin laughed. "Yank it up. Like this."

He raised the tip of his pole quickly. When he did, there was a fish on the end. Tom did the same.

"Now what do I do with it?" he asked.

His willow pole was laying on the bank beside him. The little fish, all shiny with blue and red and yellow, got dirty from flopping around in the sand. Justin looked down at it and shook his head.

"Little small, but I reckon he's keepin' size. Take him off the hook. I'll fix a stringer."

Tom felt his nose wrinkle up. "How?"

"Grab hold of him and take the hook out of his mouth."

"I don't know how."

Shaking his head, Justin walked over and picked up the fish. "You really are a city kid, aren't you? Here, I'll show you."

He took the fish off and handed the pole back to Tom.

"I ain't takin' off no more for you. Next one, you got to do by yourself. Else you'll be expecting me to take all of 'em off. Go find some more bait. I'll put these on a stringer."

"Aren't you supposed to throw 'em back in the water?"

"These are just right for eatin'. You can throw yours back if you want. I'm takin' mine home and have

Mother fix 'em up for supper. They keep biting this fast, we'll have a mess in no time."

"If that isn't the finest mess of perch I ever did see," Mama exclaimed. "Where on earth did you get them?"

Tom beamed from ear to ear. "I caught 'em myself. Even learned how to take 'em off the hook without help. Justin showed me how. We went to the fishin' hole the other side of Skeeter Ridge and—"

Mama waved her arms.

"Slow down, boy. Slow down. You're talking ninety to nothing. Back up a little bit. Now, who's this Justin you're talking about?"

"He's the boy I met yesterday."

"The one you met? You mean the one you had the fight with?"

"Yes, ma'am."

She took the fish from him and walked over to the sink.

"Glad you both decided to go fishing today instead of fighting." She glanced over her shoulder at him. "Not that your clothes look much better. What did you do—waller in the mud?"

Tom looked down at the dirt on his pants, especially around his knees.

"No, ma'am. That's the way I learned to get the fish off. I'd lay 'em down on the ground and put my knee on them so they wouldn't fin me. . . ."

The water started running in the sink.

"Go wash up. I'll clean these for you. Use some of my perfumed soap—help get the fish smell off you."

Tom scurried off up the stairs and into the tub. The perfumed soap sure had a smell to it. Tom lathered up good, then sank down under the water to get it off. "Glad Mama seems in a better mood this afternoon," he thought. "If we don't get in any more fights, maybe she'll let me and Justin spend some more time together. Maybe we can even explore Panther Peak!"

5

Over the next few weeks, it seemed like there were a million and one things Tom and Justin learned from each other. On the two days it rained, Tom taught Justin how to play chess on the little board his folks had bought him last Christmas. The day after the rain cleared, Justin met Tom down by Skeeter Creek. Justin moved slowly, taking his time to look carefully at the soft mud along the edge of the bank. There were tracks everywhere. And Justin knew what kind of animal had made each of them—where it was going, and how fast it was moving. There were so many different kinds of tracks, Tom figured he'd never learn them all. But he did manage a few of them. Rabbit tracks were easy—the long, linelike print of the hind foot and the small circles where the front feet hit. Skunk and raccoon tracks were hard to tell apart since the toes looked so much alike. But Justin explained that raccoons were usually bigger and heavier, so the tracks were usually deeper. Deer were easy to spot. And it didn't take Tom long to tell the difference between a doe and a buck. "For one thing, bucks're bigger," Justin explained. "For another, well ... look there." He pointed out a little round mark just behind the track. "Does don't have 'em. Or if they do, they ain't heavy enough to leave that kind of print."

When they weren't tracking or fishing or playing catch with the football, they snuck off to the barn and swung from the rope.

But one Saturday morning, there just wasn't anything left to do.

"Want to play catch awhile?" Tom asked.

Justin shook his head.

"How about fishin', then?"

He shook his head again.

"Bet we could catch some snakes down by the marsh."

Justin looked over the top of the comic book he was reading. "We did that yesterday." And he went back to reading the book.

Tom picked up a Superman comic. He looked at

the same picture he had already looked at five times. Suddenly, he threw the book down and leaped to his feet.

"All we been doing for the past two hours is looking at comic books. Let's do *somethin'*. This sittin' around is driving me crazy!"

Justin ignored him, at first. Then he rolled his comic up like a pirate spyglass and looked through one end of the tube. Finally, Justin got up and stood by the chair next to Tom.

"You figure we're pretty good friends?" he asked in a whisper.

"Yeah," Tom whispered back. "I haven't known you very long, but I figure you're about the best friend I've ever had."

Justin nodded. "That's the way I feel, too." He stopped to look around, then scooted closer to Tom. "Can you keep a secret? Not even tell your parents— never?"

Tom nodded quickly.

"Okay," Justin said. "But just to make sure, cross your heart and spit."

"Huh?" Tom frowned.

"Cross your heart and spit," Justin repeated.

Tom shrugged. "All right." With his finger, he made an X across his chest, then puckered up and spat.

Justin smiled. "Good," he said. Then he motioned Tom to follow. "I can't tell you the secret," he whispered. "Got to show you. Come on."

Justin said it would be a long trip, so they swiped some food from the kitchen and snuck out of the house. Once outside, they headed off toward Skeeter Ridge. Tom kept asking what the secret was, but Justin wouldn't tell him. So they just kept going.

When they got to the ridge, instead of going up the low canyon where the shortcut was, Justin turned south. They followed the base of Panther Peak for a long ways, until they reached the place where Skeeter Creek flowed through. There, they turned and started up Panther Peak. The climb was pretty easy at first; then they came to a steep rock cliff. The sides were straight and smooth as if some giant had taken an ax and sliced the bare rock clean. The creek flowed down through a narrow gorge. The boys could hear the sound of running water as it bubbled and tumbled, all white and foamy.

"This is the only way in from this side," Justin said. "Be careful. There's a lot of moss. Don't slip."

He turned sideways so he could fit into the opening of the gorge. Tom followed.

Straight rock walls towered up on either side. And in places, the top of the gorge was so narrow, the sky was hidden. There was a mist in the air from the fast-running water. The spray seemed heavy enough to drink. It made the rocks slippery and the climbing dangerous. At times they were going almost straight up, their feet just inches above the water.

It was fun for a while, but the climb became more treacherous as the rocks got more slippery. In places, the side of the gorge was so narrow, they had to turn sideways and suck in their stomachs just to squeeze through. Tom felt himself shivering. He didn't know if it was from excitement or from being downright scared.

Then, just ahead, there was an opening and the glare of the bright sun. A huge boulder blocked the end of the gorge. They had to press their backs against the wall, then claw and climb their way over it.

When Justin got to the top, he turned to help Tom. At the first sight of the place, Tom could feel himself light up like a Christmas tree.

"This is Skeeter Hole," Justin announced.

Tom could only stare, open-mouthed. Somehow, the name Skeeter Hole wasn't quite fitting for a place like this. It was kind of a plain, ordinary name—and this place was *anything* but ordinary.

Before them, on the other side of a clear, shimmering pool, was a waterfall. It wasn't a big one—only about ten feet high and maybe five feet across—but it was still a waterfall. It made a soft rumbling sound as the water spilled over the rock ledge above and tumbled, all white, into the pool. The pool itself was about twenty feet around—almost a perfect circle. On either side, the cliffs rose straight and smooth. The boulder they stood on served as a dam to hold the water in. And looking down into the water, Tom could see every stone and pebble.

"You swim here?" Tom asked.

Justin nodded. "Yeah. That's one of the reasons I made you promise never to tell. If Mother and Dad knew I went swimming without them there to watch, they'd skin me alive."

Tom shook his head. "Yeah. I know what you mean. That's the way my folks are. I've been swimming since I was five and they still don't think I know how."

Justin starting unbuttoning his shirt. "You want to go in?"

"What if our parents find out?"

"Well, I'm sure not gonna tell them. Are you?"

"No."

"This place is over two miles from my house, and the only way in is there by the falls. I dug out some footholes with a rock last summer. Grownups are too big to get through that gorge—the way we came up. So nobody's gonna find out." He threw his shirt down on the big boulder and kicked his shoes off.

"We'll leave our clothes here on the rock so they don't get wet. They'll never know we've even been near the water, much less swimming in it."

It took no time at all to shuck their clothes. The sun was hot on their backs. The more Tom looked at the cool, clear water, the hotter the sun seemed to get and the more he wanted to dive in.

He threw his hands back and bent over to dive, but Justin stopped him.

"Not here. Follow me. I'll show you how to get in."

They moved to the left, following a narrow ledge, just wide enough for their feet. On the near side of the pool was a sandbar, just barely under the surface of the water. A huge cottonwood grew in its center, and a big rope hung from one of its lower branches. Its loose end dangled on the water, tracing a path over the mirrorlike surface as the slight breath of wind pushed it to and fro.

Justin waded out and got the rope. "I brought this rope here about two years ago," he called over his shoulder. Then, bringing it back, he climbed the ledge where Tom waited.

"You think swinging from the loft is fun, watch this."

He tucked up his knees, then swooped from the ledge like an eagle diving for its prey. Out, out to the very center of the shimmering blue pool and up, up into the clear, bright sky. At the very top of his swing, he let go.

Legs churning, arms wheeling around like a windmill, he fell to the water with a splash that sent a spray in all directions. Water glistened where it hit the sides of the cliffs. Tom could feel the cool droplets on his bare feet.

Laughing and sputtering, Justin came back to the surface. When the rope stopped swinging, he grabbed it and flung it to Tom.

"Just remember to let go," he called. "You swing backwards into that cliff you're on, you'll bash yourself up."

Tom could feel his knees trembling as he clutched the rope in his hand. He glanced down. His knuckles were white.

It was scary, being up here like this. The cliff where he stood was a long way from the water. And right below him was that sandbar, only an inch or two under the surface. If he slipped and hit that . . . Tom felt himself quiver.

Looking out over the pool was even worse. The place where the rope stopped swinging was right over the center of the pool, and very high up.

"Come on," Justin called.

Tom took a deep breath. He couldn't chicken out. Not with Justin watching.

He closed his eyes.

Squeezed the rope.

Jumped.

Tom didn't open his eyes again until right before he hit the water. Like Justin, his legs and arms were spinning in all directions. He could feel himself falling.

The water was like ice. It almost knocked the breath from his lungs. He fought his way back to the surface, gasping for air.

But instead of being scared, the first thing he heard was himself laughing. Laughing as loud as he could. He'd never felt so free. So alive.

"That's great," he squealed. "Let's go again."

Justin splashed some water at him. "There's somethin' else I got to show you, first." Treading water, he motioned Tom to follow. "Come on."

They swam across the center of the pool, straight for the falls.

Justin swam right under it.

Tom stopped, treading water and watching.

From the other side of the roaring water, he heard Justin's voice: "Come on!"

Tom grabbed a deep breath. Slowly, he swam into the falling water.

The roar under the falls was so loud, he couldn't hear anything else. The water pounded all about him. It beat his head and stung as it hit his shoulders in white, heavy sheets. The spray was so thick, he could barely see. The water was heavy in the air, and he could barely catch his breath.

Then he was in a cave—a dark, green, mossy cave. There was a still pool behind the falls, about six feet around. Above it was a little ledge. The ceiling reflected a blue-green light from the falls. It danced and changed shapes, making the cave mysterious-looking, like something seen in a misty dream.

Justin sat on the ledge, a few feet above the water. "Over yonder." He pointed. "There're some rocks under the water where you can climb up."

It was cool in here. A clean smell came from the water. Droplets fell from the moss on the ceiling, like a soft spring shower.

"I don't believe it," Tom whispered. The sound of the falls was quieter here, but it still drummed in his ears. "I don't believe it," he repeated.

It was a private world. A place that no one else knew about. A place where they could do or be anything or anyone they wanted. There was no one to watch, no one to giggle and say, "Aren't they cute little kids." There were no grownups to make fun of them or tell them what to do or what not to do. This was Justin and Tom's place. Their secret place.

After sitting in the cave, they swam back out and swung from the rope. They played until they were tired and hot from the bright sun that shone down, then swam back under the falls to rest in the cave.

Tom closed his eyes. He let one foot dangle over the ledge and slosh in the cool water. The sound of the falls was like a giant drum—or the rumbling and pounding of a mean thunderstorm building in the distance.

The two boys were quiet for a while. Then, just barely above the sound of the waterfall, Tom heard a growling sound. He sat up, looking at his stomach. It growled again, and that reminded him. "Justin?" He shook his friend's leg. "You hungry?"

"Yeah."

Tom rolled off his rock like a turtle rolling off a stump. "I'll go get the food we brought. We can eat in here."

He swam under the pounding falls and across the pool to the boulder where they had left their clothes.

In the middle of the pool he stopped. He didn't

know why. There was a strange feeling, like eyes were staring at the back of his neck.

He treaded water. Looked around.

There was nothing there. Nothing at all, not even the birds that had been chirping and scampering about in the big cottonwood when they'd first arrived. The stillness made the feeling even worse.

Tom shook his head. "I'm just imagining things," he told himself. "There's nobody looking at me. Nobody even knows about this place."

In a moment the feeling passed and he swam on to get the apples and grapes from his pants pocket.

The boulder was too far to reach from the water. But just next to it was a rock ledge. Tom pulled himself up, bracing his feet on the ledge so he wouldn't slip, and reached out to feel around for his clothes.

His hand found the clothes, but there was something else. . . .

He could hear it.

He held his breath. Froze.

He could hear a sort of soft breathing sound. Then another sound. Something was moving. Walking through the brush.

"Who's there?"

The sound was moving away.

"Who's up there?"

Whatever or whoever it was was getting farther away. Tom raised his foot to a knob of rock on the boulder. He took a firm hold of the clothes with one hand. With the other, he felt around for another rough spot in the rock so he'd have a good handhold. When he finally found one, he pulled himself up and peeked over the boulder.

There was nothing there. "Must be my imagination." He shrugged.

He started searching through the armload of clothes for the food they'd brought from the house.

Then . . . that strange feeling came over him again. That feeling like there were eyes staring at him. Watching him.

He froze. Held his breath. Nothing moved but his eyes.

Suddenly, it *was* there—looking at him.

There was a large rock about thirty feet away. Beside it, he could see a square head. Black—like the night sky. Yellow-green eyes stared straight at him. Cold eyes that seemed to cut clear down inside him.

Tom screamed.

The cold eyes blinked.

There was a sudden flash, like lightning moving across the sky—only this lightning was black. Black as death itself.

Four legs. A long, sleek body. A tail.

That's all he saw before the animal disappeared behind the rock.

Tom's eyes flashed.

"Panther!" The word whooshed from his lips. Then he yelled and fell backward.

Before he knew it, he was swimming toward the falls. Swimming as hard as he could. Afraid to look back, afraid that the cat—whatever he had seen— might leap on him at any second.

Justin heard him yelling the second he swam under the falls.

"What is it, Tom?" he shouted back. "What's wrong?"

"Out there," he gasped. "That thing. Big! Out there."

Justin was on his feet. He took Tom's arm and pulled him from the water.

"What thing? Where? What is it?"

Tom had never swum so hard in his life. He was out of breath.

"Near the rock . . . by our clothes . . . cat . . . big . . ."

Justin took him by the shoulders and shook him.

"What kind of cat?"

"Don't know . . . black . . . looked like . . . like a . . . panther."

"A panther!!"

Justin looked toward the falls.

"Wait here." He dived into the water and swam from the cave.

"No!" Tom screamed.

But Justin didn't hear. He was already under the falls.

Tom huddled down in a corner of the cave, shaking and trembling.

6

It seemed like Justin would never come back. He was gone forever. But finally Tom saw him swim under the falls. He came up by the ledge where Tom was. He spit out some water he'd swallowed.

"There's nothing out there."

Tom tried to stop shaking. He couldn't.

"Yes, there is. I saw it. It's there!"

"But I looked all over the place." Justin glared at him. "There ain't nothin'. Are you sure you saw a panther?"

Tom swallowed. "I . . . I think so."

"Then where is it? If you really saw something, show me."

Tom shook his head.

"No!"

Justin climbed up on the ledge and tugged at his arm. "Show me. Show me where you saw it. Maybe we can find some tracks."

"No!"

Tom yanked his arm away from Justin's grasp. He tucked himself up into a ball and sat back in the corner of the cave. Above him, he could see Justin staring. The way the light shone on his face made his eyes look dark and mean. The corners of his mouth were turned way down.

"I really saw it," he told Justin in almost a whisper. "I swear."

The mean look left Justin's face. He sat beside Tom and sighed softly.

"I believe you. But . . . well . . ." He tilted his head to the side. "There are lots of animals around here. But there ain't no panthers or mountain lions or nothin' like that. I don't see why you're so scared about it. Besides, whatever you thought you saw is gone now. If you show me where it was, maybe we can find some tracks and figure out what kind of animal it was."

They swam under the falls. Tom stopped in the middle of the pool. He treaded water and listened. Looked all around.

The birds were back. He could hear their chirping and see them fluttering about in the big cottonwood.

"You're right," he told Justin. "Whatever it was is gone now."

He led the way toward the boulder. The sun had moved far to the west. The whole pool was in the shade. On the face of the other cliff, long shadows told them that it would be dark before long. If they were going to find out what it was, they had to hurry.

"Up there." Tom pointed. "When I started to get the food out of my pants, I saw it."

Justin climbed to the little ridge at the edge of the boulder. Tom could hear him groan as he strained and tugged his way up.

Finally, he managed to pull himself to the top of the huge rock.

"I don't see anything," he called.

"It was by that big rock, about thirty feet to the right."

Justin disappeared over the boulder. Tom could hear him moving around, rattling the bushes and mumbling to himself.

"There's nothing over here," he called. "No tracks at all."

"It could have climbed the rocks," Tom said. "It wouldn't leave any tracks that way."

In a minute, Justin was back, standing on the rock and looking down. His eyes were real tight. His lips were pressed close together, like he was fixing to bust.

"Like I said," Justin repeated in a growl. "There's nothin' up here. Nothin' except this."

He stooped down and picked up one of Tom's tennis shoes.

Puzzled, Tom frowned.

"That's all?"

Justin nodded. "That's *all!*"

He threw the tennis shoe in the water.

"Hey," Tom yelled. "What did you do that for?"

Justin glared at him. "Might as well get everything wet."

"Everything? You mean the other stuff . . ."

"That's right," Justin cut him off. "*Everything*. I can see part of it, right there by your feet."

Tom looked down. Sure enough—shirts, shoes, pants—everything was there in the water beside him. Justin folded his arms and stared down.

"I just figured out what happened. You saw a skunk or a raccoon, or some kind of little animal—and since you're a city kid, it scared you and you dropped the clothes. Then, so I wouldn't get mad at you, you made up that story about seein' some big, scary panther."

Frantically, Tom shook his head. "No . . . I really saw it. And it wasn't little, either. It was big and black and it had yellow-green eyes—like a cat. When I saw it, I must have jumped and dropped the clothes, trying to get away."

But Justin only nodded. No matter how many times Tom tried to apologize, it seemed like Justin never would forgive him for throwing all their clothes in the water.

They talked and argued, but their conversation didn't last long. The tall shadows had already fallen across the pool. The darkness was beginning to settle in. They had to get home before their parents came looking for them.

"You've really done it now," Justin said as he fished his shirt from the bottom of the pool. "There ain't no way we're gonna get these clothes dried out before we get home. Our folks are gonna know we been in swimming. Man, are we gonna catch it!"

After they spent nearly half an hour diving for their clothes, there was still one thing they couldn't find— Tom's pants.

"I can't go home without my pants," Tom moaned. "Mama'll kill me, sure."

Justin looked up at the sky. "It's getting dark, Tom. We can't stay here any longer. We got to go."

"But my pants—"

"We got to go," Justin repeated.

It was night before Tom made it home. The wind had settled for a time, right before he got to the barn. Then it came up again, from the northwest—a cool breeze that raced along in front of tall, blue-black clouds that formed a cool front. There wasn't any rain, not yet, but it didn't make any difference since Tom was soaking wet anyway.

Tom shivered. The yard lamp gave off enough light for him to see. He leaned against the side of the corral. He wrapped his arms around himself. There were lights coming from the living room and the kitchen.

"Just my luck," he thought. "Can't even sneak in through the back door. And I can't wait out here in the dark very long, either. I got wet shoes, and a wet shirt and wet underwear, and no pants. I'll freeze to death.

"They're probably already worried about me. If I could just get in the back door and get up to my room, I could put on some dry clothes and hide these and . . ."

The light in the kitchen went off. Tom strained his eyes, leaning far out around the corner of the barn. He couldn't see anybody in the kitchen. "They must all be in the living room watching TV," he told himself. "Now's my chance."

He ran across the barnyard as fast as he could go. His wet tennis shoes made a sloshing sound as he moved. When he got to the back door, he took them off. He waved his feet, trying to dry them enough so he wouldn't leave tracks on the floor. There was talking from the living room, but Tom didn't listen. He was concentrating on the steps.

If he had been listening, he would have heard his mother's voice saying: "I'm so glad you came." And his father saying, "Tom should be home by now. I can't imagine what's happened to him." And Mrs. Riley, who would be his new teacher when school started, answering, "I always like to visit the homes of my new students. I'm so sorry I missed Tom."

"Would you like some more coffee?" his mother asked.

"Yes," answered Mrs. Riley. "Let me go with you."

It was right at that moment when Tom closed the screen door behind him. He started across the kitchen floor on tiptoes. When he got in the middle of the kitchen, the door flew open. His mother's voice said, "Do you take cream in your coffee, Mrs. Riley?"

And the light came on.

Tom froze in his tracks. His mother's eyes flew open. Mrs. Riley's mouth flew open. Tom started to run, but fell over the table.

"Tom," his mother screamed. "What on earth—"

He was on the floor now, looking up at the two women.

"Where are your pants?" his mother cried. Mrs.

Riley turned and left the kitchen instantly. And Tom took off up the stairs as hard as he could go.

He knew what was going to happen. But he couldn't do anything about it. He'd promised Justin he would never tell.

All in all, it was a rotten way to end the summer. He couldn't believe that Mrs. Riley, his new teacher, had come to visit, especially on the very night he lost his pants in Skeeter Hole. And he couldn't believe that she and his mother had come in the kitchen to get some coffee just as he walked in the door. It was embarrassing—the most embarrassing thing that had ever happened to Tom.

What he *could* believe was that they grounded him for a whole month. It was hard to take—not being able to see Justin or go out and play—but he figured he deserved it. Besides, there wasn't much he could do about it.

The thing that really worried him was starting school. Monday was Labor Day and school would start on Tuesday.

"What if I go into my new room, on the very first day at a new school, and Mrs. Riley smiles at me and says something like, 'Oh, Tom Burke. I'm glad you remembered your pants.'"

Tom felt his eyes roll. "If she does something like that, I'll die! I'll just flat die!"

7

Tom felt like he held his breath the whole, entire first day of school. Every time Mrs. Riley looked at him, he could feel his face turning red.

Only, Mrs. Riley never said anything about the night she came to visit. Tom was on edge about it for the first few days of school, but after that, he figured that Mrs. Riley was "an all right lady" and he didn't have to worry.

Justin never said anything either. Tom had been afraid he'd say something about Tom seeing some kind of little animal and thinking it was a panther—but he didn't.

Being grounded wasn't all that bad. Tom found out that Justin was grounded, too. So they were both stuck. For the whole month of September, the only time they got to see each other was on the bus and at recess. When Tom got home after school, he had to go to the barn or the corral to help his dad and grandfather with the chores. It was the same thing on weekends.

If there was anything good about the whole mess, it was Susan. Now that he was grounded, she seemed to be a whole lot nicer. Maybe she felt sorry for him or something—Tom didn't know. But she did seem easier to get along with. She even played checkers and stuff with him a few times.

On September 25, Tom's birthday, he woke up at least expecting to smell the aroma of a cake baking in the oven. Only, when he sat up in bed and sniffed the air, there was nothing.

He got dressed real quick and scurried into Mama and Dad's room. Back home, they always hid his presents in their closet. He looked in and scooted some of the shoes and stuff around.

There was nothing there. No boxes. No wrapping paper or bright bows.

Tom walked down the stairs with his head hung low like a whipped pup. "Guess being grounded includes birthdays, too," he muttered.

He kicked up a lot of dust as he shuffled across the dark barnyard and went to help Grampa with the morning milking. When they were finished, Grampa puffed on his pipe and looked out the barn door.

"It's gonna be a rough one. Yep. All the signs for a rough winter. Could be as bad as the winter of 1933."

Tom took the bucket of fresh milk from under Old Josie and poured it into the big cooler.

"Wasn't that the year you saw the panther, Grampa?"

Grampa nodded. Tom handed him the milk bucket so he could rinse it out in the sink.

"Reckon it might be a bad enough winter that a panther might come back to Panther Peak?"

Grampa was sloshing water around in the milk bucket and didn't seem to hear. Tom started to ask again about the possibility of panthers returning to Panther Peak. He wanted to tell Grampa about what he'd seen—or thought he'd seen—at Skeeter Hole. He thought on it a minute, then decided it was best to forget the whole thing, and turned his attention back to the cow.

Old Josie was a pretty good milk cow. She gave a lot of milk and she didn't try to kick like some of the others.

Tom petted her a minute, then turned her into the feedlot, where she could eat some hay.

"That's all of 'em, Grampa. We're through milking."

Grampa turned to him with a smile. "You mean

we've milked all ten of those cows already? My, my, doesn't seem like we've been out here that long."

Tom rubbed his hands together, trying to warm them up. Then he reached in his pocket for his gloves.

"We learned in geography class that it gets warmer the farther south you go. Is that right?"

Grampa nodded. "Yep. That's the way it usually works."

They walked to the ladder that led to the hayloft and started up.

"Then how come it's colder here than it is in Enid? Enid is farther north than we are, and it doesn't get this cold around there until the last part of November. It should be warm here."

Grampa rolled a bale of hay from the loft.

"Usually is," he answered. "We're just in for a rough winter. Looks like it's come early this year, too. September's usually more like summer, but we're already getting chilly nights and cool days. We're gonna be in for some weather, all right."

Tom helped him with the second bale. They pushed and shoved until it tipped over the edge of the loft and fell with a thud to the barn floor.

"Come on," Grampa said. "I got something to show you."

They climbed down from the loft and Grampa took his pliers and cut the two strands of bailing wire on one of the hay bales. "Grab a couple of blocks from that bale and fetch it for me."

Tom got two chunks of hay and followed his grand-father.

They went around on the far side of the barn, where Grampa opened the gate to a pen.

"Pitch that block of hay in there," he said.

Standing right in front of them was a horse.

Tom's mouth flopped open.

"That's a horse, Grampa."

"I know what it is," Grampa growled. "Throw her some hay. She's hungry."

"But we don't have a horse, Grampa."

Grampa chuckled. "You just told me it was a horse. Now, throw her the hay."

"But . . . but Grampa . . . where did it come from?"

Grampa took the block of hay out of Tom's arms and pitched it into the pen. The horse reached down and started eating.

She was a beautiful buckskin mare with a dark brown stripe down her back. Tom frowned as he watched her eat.

"Where did she come from, Grampa?" he repeated. "I was just around here, after we finished milking last night. There wasn't a horse here, then."

Grampa struck a match on his overalls. Puffed at his pipe.

"Your dad and I went after her while you were sleep-in'. You like her?"

Tom felt a chill shoot up his back.

"Well . . . sure . . . she's beautiful. . . ."

Grampa smiled so big that his pipe almost fell out of his mouth. "I'm glad to hear that," he said. Then he turned toward the barn and waved. "I'm glad you like her, 'cause . . . she's yours."

Mama and Dad and Susan all came out of the barn then, singing "Happy Birthday." Mama was carrying a cake, and when they got finished singing, everybody started talking and laughing and everything, all at once.

Tom could only stand there like a dummy with his mouth hanging open. He was so surprised, he ended up leaning against the corral and hanging onto a fence post, just to keep from crumpling up on the ground.

When he finally got over the shock, he couldn't hold still. He got to fidgeting and wiggling and shuffling from one foot to the other.

"Is she really mine?" He said it over and over, and each time he did, Grampa and Dad and Mama and Susan would nod and get to laughing again.

"I'm gonna name her Ginger."

He climbed over the fence and went to pet her, then he climbed down and ate some of the birthday cake Mama and Susan dished up on paper plates. Then he went back and petted her some more and then had some more cake.

"She's expecting a baby, too," Grampa told him.

"Really!" Tom squealed. "You mean I'm gonna have two horses?"

Grampa nodded.

"When?"

"Late February. Maybe early March."

"How come she's due to foal so early?" Dad interrupted.

Grampa took a long puff on his pipe and shook his head.

"Old boy we bought her from fancies himself as a racehorse breeder. His idea is that if he gets the mares to drop their foals in February or March, that gives them longer to grow, so by the time they're two-year-olds and ready for the track, they'll be bigger than the others."

Grampa shook his head again.

"I don't hold with it. Late March or April, the grass is out and the mare's got lots more food. A February foal might be a couple of months older, but one born in April grows faster and is usually healthier. Lose a lot of foals in cold weather, too."

Tom felt his eyebrows raise.

"You think we might lose Ginger's baby, Grampa?"

68   DANGER ON PANTHER PEAK

"No. We'll keep her up in the corral. Come time for her to foal, we'll put her in the barn where it's warm and dry. She'll be all right. Thing she needs now is regular feed and plenty of exercise. Reckon I could talk you into ridin' her?"

Tom felt his face light up like the bulb on a Christmas tree. Then his chest and shoulders sagged.

"I'm still grounded."

Dad gave a little chuckle. "Well . . . figure since Grampa needs that mare exercised . . . well, I reckon we can count it as helping with the chores instead of playing."

"All right!" Tom yelled.

It only took them a few seconds to get the saddle and bridle on her. Tom rode her around the corral for a minute or two, just to get used to handling her. She turned easy and stopped quick, and just the slightest pressure from his heels took her to a slow, easy lope.

After a few times around the corral, Dad opened the gate. Tom rode over to him and stopped.

Dad smiled at him.

"Reckon if you ride her out to the far end of Skeeter Ridge, you just might find somebody to ride with."

"Justin?"

Dad's smile got bigger. He reached up and patted Tom's knee.

"Yeah. Happy birthday."

Tom swallowed the lump in his throat.

"Thank you, Dad. It's the best birthday *ever*."

Tom and Justin found that they liked riding together just about as much as playing together. Most of October was warm and pretty, so they rode almost every day, after school and all day on Saturdays.

The far end of Skeeter Ridge was a long ride from Grampa's house, so the second Saturday in November, Justin got his dad's pruning saw and they started working on a path near the shortcut at the base of Panther Peak. They left the horses home, that Saturday, and walked the shortcut on foot, to make sure it was safe for the horses. They checked for any holes or big cracks in the rocks for the animals to step in and hurt their legs. Then they took the saw and cut branches out of the way so they could ride through the narrow places without having to get off and walk.

They were both tired and hot and sweaty by the time evening came.

"We got it done," Justin said as he sank down in the tall brown grass. "It'll only take about twenty minutes to get from my house to yours, now that we got us a horse trail by the shortcut."

Tom nodded and sank down beside him.

"Sure was hard work. But now we'll have twice as much time to ride or play, since we don't have to go clean to the end of the ridge and come around."

Only trouble was, they just got to use the trail a couple of times before the cold weather that Grampa had predicted set in. It was so windy and nasty cold that Tom didn't want to go out and help with the chores, much less saddle Ginger and go riding. He'd ride her around the corral, to exercise her, like Grampa wanted, but it was just too cold to go across the prairie or toward the ridge.

He went over to Justin's house a few times on the weekends, and Justin had his parents drive him over to Tom's a couple of times. But aside from that, winter put a screeching halt to all their playing and having fun outside.

8

The second week of January, it turned real cold. A light snow came, but there wasn't enough to even cover the tall tufts of love grass in the pasture. It stayed so cold, though, that the little dab of snow was on the ground for a long time.

The first week in February, it warmed up a bit, but the very next night, another snow came. This one wasn't any deeper than the first, but the freezing weather that came with it seemed even worse.

Ever since the cold weather set in, Dad had been helping Grampa with the morning milking. Tom still helped out in the afternoons, but without morning chores he got to sleep late most Saturdays. It was the one nice thing about weekends—not having to get up early and do chores or go to school. But the third Saturday in February, he got to tossing and turning in bed. No matter what he did, he couldn't get warm. Even with the pillow over his head, it seemed bright in the room. Bright, like Mama had turned on the light or something.

Tom fought waking up by tucking himself up in a little ball in the middle of the bed. But finally, he realized it was no use. There was no way he could get back to sleep.

He yawned, threw back the covers, and got up.

The second his feet touched the wood floor, he jumped back in the bed and pulled the covers over him.

"That floor's like stepping in a pan of ice," he thought. He was good and awake after that.

Despite the icy floor, Tom got up and walked quickly to the window. He flung open the curtains.

There was a blanket of white everywhere. It shimmered and glistened like the sparkles in his mother's wedding ring. The evergreens at the side of his window spread their limbs, burdened with the heavy snow, looking like any moment they'd drop their white load and spring back, throwing the white powder high into the clear, blue sky.

It took a total of five minutes for Tom to brush his teeth, wash his face, get dressed, and race down to the breakfast table.

Everybody was already there, except for Susan. Steam came from Dad's and Grampa's coffee cups. And while they stirred their coffee with a spoon in one hand, both men held their other hands above the steam, like they were warming their hands at a fire. Mama was busy at the stove.

Tom licked his lips. Already he could smell bacon and eggs and the fresh biscuits she was cooking for breakfast.

"Did you see it?" He raced to the kitchen door, to make sure the snow was really out there and he hadn't just been dreaming. "Did you see the snow?"

"You're up mighty early for a Saturday," his father called.

"Did you see the snow, Dad? When did it come?"

His father chuckled. "Started around eleven last night. From the looks of things, it probably kept coming down until daybreak."

"How deep is it? Can I go out? Where's the sled? Will you pull me?"

He was so excited, he grabbed his father's arm and shook it. The coffee sloshed around in his cup. A little spilled.

"Hey, slow down." His dad laughed. "Eat your breakfast. Then we'll talk about going out."

"I'm not lookin' foward to gettin' out in this stuff,"

Grampa said, lighting his pipe. "But Sally didn't show up for milking this morning. We're gonna have to go hunt her. Might as well take Tom along."

Dad blew into his cup.

"I thought we were one short at milking time," he agreed. "Should have figured it was Sally. She's due to drop her calf sometime this week or next. Guess she lit out for a hiding place."

"You mean she's gonna have a calf out in the cold and snow?" Tom felt his eyes pop. "Won't she freeze?"

Dad shook his head. "She won't. But chances are, if we don't find her soon, that calf of hers might be in trouble."

"Then why'd she do it?" Tom asked. "She's got a warm barn out there and plenty of hay. Why'd she want to run off to have her calf?"

"Hanged if I know." Dad shook his head. "How about you, Grampa?"

Grampa puffed at his pipe. "Just the way with an old cow. They always like to go off alone to have their calf. Go off and hide. Should have locked her up, only I figured we had a while longer before she was ready."

"I'll help you find her," Tom announced. "I'll run up and get my stocking cap and my boots and then I'll—"

"Hold on just a minute, young squirt." Mama shook the skillet of scrambled eggs. "That snow's not going anyplace, and neither are you till breakfast is eaten."

"But Mama—"

Grampa reached out and gave him a playful swat on the bottom. "Your mother's right. This here snow's liable to stay quite a while. No sense gettin' in no big rush."

Tom sat down with a sigh. "Do you really think it will last, Grampa? Will it?"

"Just liable to. When your dad and I went to milk, the temperature was fifteen above. I don't remember it bein' that cold, with snow on the ground, since way back around . . . well, it was 1929—or was it 1928 . . . no, it was . . . well, it was 1933, sure as I'm sittin' here," Grampa went on. "That's the year that big cat almost got me and Slim. Don't know how I could ever forget that. It was the same year that the big snow come. Never seen anything like it, probably never will again." He turned to Dad. "Charlie, you remember your grandmother?"

Dad nodded.

"She sure was a spunky little woman," Grampa went on. Then to Tom: "That'd be your great-grandmother, Tom. She died before you were born.

"Why, I remember . . . not long after that cat tried to get me and Slim, it came down and tried to get the calves. Your great-grandmother saw him, one evening about sundown. She grabbed that old double-barreled ten-gauge shotgun I got up under the bed and took after that cat. He seen her comin' and lit out for the hills. But she dusted his tail good. Never did come back chasing our calves.

"The hunters took him off Panther Peak about two months after that. He was *one, big* cat! The boys brought that fresh-killed panther past the house. Them sure is mean-lookin' animals."

Grampa looked off at the ceiling, remembering.

"Yep. Your great-grandmother was sure a spunky little woman, all right. She was about the best mother a man could ever have. Why, I remember one time . . ."

He kept right on talking, clear through breakfast. Tom liked listening to his grandfather's stories about the old days. He didn't eat much because he was so busy listening.

Dad liked listening to Grampa's stories, too, but when he finished breakfast and downed his third cup of coffee, he pushed his chair back from the table.

"We best go feed the stock, Grampa. We'll see if we can find Sally, while we're out."

Tom felt a smile stretch the corners of his mouth.

"Dad? Can you pull me on the sled? Can you pull me behind the truck?"

Mama took a stack of dirty dishes to the sink. "Pullin' a sled behind the pickup is dangerous," she said over her shoulder.

Dad smiled back at Tom. "I'll be going slow, dear," he answered. "Why not let Tom ride his sled?"

"Now, Charlie." Mama shook her finger at Dad. "You might near had that boy froze last year when you took him out on the sled while we were visiting Grampa. I rubbed on his hands and feet until I was near tuckered out. I'll not have it again."

Dad looked at Tom. Then he looked at Mama. Then he looked back at Tom.

"I won't let him get that cold, Amanda." Dad talked real soft to Mama, like he usually did when he wanted her to let him do something. "If Tom starts getting cold, I'll make him get in the truck. All right, dear?"

Mama was still frowning. So Dad walked over and took hold of her. Then he tried to kiss her. She put up a fuss at first. Only she didn't fight very hard. Then they were kissing and sort of giggling.

"Grownups sure act goofy," Tom thought. "Sure hope I don't act like that when I grow up."

Dad reached over and ruffled Tom's hair. "Come on."

Only, Mama grabbed Dad by his back pocket.

"But what if you have to stop fast, Charlie? What if that sled slides up under the pickup?"

Tom stepped in to help his Dad out. "I won't get

hurt, Mama. I know how to fall off. I won't slide under the truck."

"See?" Dad winked at her. "Tom knows how to ride a sled. He knows how to fall off, too, don't you, son?"

"We'll be careful, Mom," Tom pleaded. "Please? Pretty please?"

"All right." She popped at them with her dish towel. "But if you get hurt, don't come crying to me."

Tom and his dad smiled at each other. Still smiling, they took off for the back door before Mama could change her mind.

On the top step, Tom stopped and cupped a hand to his mouth.

"You coming, Grampa?"

From inside he could hear: "Might go. Might not. It's awful cold out there."

"I'll get the rope to tie you on, son," Dad called.

Tom raced for the barn. It took some prowling and climbing over stuff, but he finally got to the back of the little room where the sled was. It was brown and rough-looking because the paint had worn off from all the times he'd used it. The metal runners were rusty on the sides, but he'd made sure that before he put it up, the bottom of the runners were smooth and bright so the sled would go better on the snow.

It took considerable pushing and pulling, grunting

and groaning, but he managed to get the sled over all the other junk in the room. He dragged it to the door.

Dad was waiting at the truck with a long brown rope. He tied one end to a steel bar at the back of the truck under the fender. The other end he tied to the middle brace on Tom's sled.

"Stay in the middle," Dad cautioned. "Don't want you getting wrapped up in that rope."

There was a sound behind them. The screen door slammed and Grampa came waddling out into the cold winter morning.

"Amanda said I best go with you. Says you can't look for old Sally and keep an eye on Tom at the same time."

Dad chuckled. "Mama worries too much. Climb in," he added, opening the door for Grampa. Then to Tom: "If we have to stop, drag your feet so the sled won't run up under us. If you can't stop, roll off. Snow'll hurt a lot less than the rear end of this truck."

"I'll be careful, Dad." Tom stretched out on the sled and held on to the wood bar across the front, just above the runners.

"Let's go!"

The pickup made a grinding sound when Dad turned it on. A pile of white steam came bellowing out the tail pipe. When the smoke cleared, Tom could see his grandfather watching him out the window of the truck.

Tom nodded that he was ready. Grampa tapped Dad on the shoulder and the truck started moving.

Tom watched the rope play out. When it sprung taut, the sled jerked, jumping forward. He hung tight to the wood.

Dad drove real slow. The pickup seemed to just barely creep along. It wasn't much fun, going this slow, so Tom waved for him to go faster. Grampa was watching. He only laughed. Dad kept the pickup at a crawl.

But when they got out of the barnyard—out of sight of the house and Mama—Dad really opened her up.

The truck made a roaring sound. The tires spun around in the snow, kicking some of it clear back on Tom. The rope that pulled the sled seemed to sing as it popped tight. And they were off.

The cold wind bit at Tom's nose and cheeks. The air made his hair stand on end. They were really moving. The snow whizzed past beneath the sled. When Tom glanced over his shoulder, he could see the white powder shooting high in the air behind him.

"We must be going sixty," he thought. "Maybe even faster."

Everything was a blur. The ground streaked past under him. The trees and the fence posts seemed like brown dots against the white background.

He loved the feeling of going fast. The smooth,

gliding feel as the sled skimmed over the soft snow. The feel of the wind against his face. Going down a hill on a sled was fun. But being pulled by a truck— going really fast, like he was now—that was great!

The pickup slowed. Some cows stood close by. They were all bunched up together, trying to keep warm. Their breath came out in white steam.

Dad pulled the truck up next to them and stopped. The sled kept moving, but not very fast. Tom was pretty sure he wasn't going fast enough to slide into the back of the truck. But just to make sure, he dragged one foot, bringing the sled to a stop.

Dad threw out some hay. The cows didn't even act like they saw it. They were all staring at Tom and the sled. They gave little snorts and pawed at the snow.

Dad started the pickup moving again. And as soon as they were gone, the cows came up to the hay and started eating. Dad drove to the next bunch of cows, while Tom hung to the sled at the end of the rope.

After all the cows were fed, Dad started driving along the far edge of Skeeter Ridge, looking for Sally. It was hard going. They had to move slowly because there were big rocks half buried under the snow— gullies that Dad couldn't see from inside the truck until he was right on top of them. They followed the ridge.

"Keep a sharp eye out," Grampa called from the truck. "Old cows can hide pretty good in these trees."

Tom sat up so he could see better. He squinted into the dark, patchy shadows of the big trees. It was hard to see—dark under the trees and blinding white in the sunlight. But Tom looked carefully. Sally just wasn't there.

The ridge was nearly a mile long, before it came to the little low spot that marked the shortcut between it and Panther Peak. The peak towered upward in front of the truck. The sheer rock cliff near the top that looked like a giant, flat-topped fortress loomed above them.

"I sure hope they don't stop close to here," Tom thought. "If Grampa finds those tree limbs Justin and I cut off, he'll know we been up here messing around, and after all the warnings he's given me about Panther Peak, he never would forgive me."

Tom gave a little sigh of relief as they drove past the horse trail.

All of a sudden, the pickup stopped.

Tom felt the sled still going. He glanced up and saw the tail pipe at the rear of the pickup coming straight for him. He leaned to the side and fell off the sled just before it hit the back of the truck.

He got up slowly and dusted the snow from his pants and coat. His face was cold and wet, and some of the snow was packed down inside his shirt. It was really cold. Tom unbuttoned his coat and dug it out.

He expected Dad and Grampa to come running back to see if he was all right. But when he looked up, he saw them running toward a clump of blackjack trees at the edge of the peak.

At his age, Grampa wasn't much for running, especially on slippery snow. But the way he was moving now, Tom knew there was trouble. He forgot about dusting the rest of the snow off and raced after the two men.

9

He followed them through the trees, dodging back and forth, ducking under limbs and climbing over dead and fallen branches. Some of the branches were ones that Tom and Justin had cut to make their trail, only Dad and Grampa never noticed. Up ahead of him, they had stopped at a place where a bunch of brush, laden down with snow, was piled up. And there, under the side of the windbreak, was Sally and her calf—what was left of them, anyway.

Tom just got a glimpse of what Dad and Grampa were looking at. Still, he felt sick. He stayed back a ways, turning his head to keep from throwing up.

Sally was dead. Something had killed her. All

around the cow, where the snow should have been white and crisp and clean, there was red from the blood that had drained from her.

The calf was a little ways off. There were tracks in the snow where something had dragged it away from its mama. The calf was even worse-looking than Sally.

Tom glanced at the sight once more. It was the most horrible thing he could ever think of. Poor old Sally, and that little baby of hers. Tom almost wanted to cry.

Dad and Grampa didn't say anything. They just stood there and looked. After a minute or so, Grampa walked over to where the calf was. Real slow, he knelt down and looked at something in the snow. It was a track of some kind. He traced around it with his finger, frowning, like he usually did when he was trying hard to remember something.

Then, like lightning, he was on his feet again, moving toward Dad and Tom.

"Hurry," he yelled, "get to the truck!"

Puzzled, they stared at him.

"Get to the truck! *Now!*"

There wasn't much that scared Tom's grandfather. The fact was, Tom had never known the old man to be afraid of anything. But when Grampa called out the second time, Tom heard the terror in his voice and knew that something had scared his Grampa—bad.

He lit out for the truck at a dead run. Dad and Grampa were right behind him.

Tom didn't know what he was running from, or why. He was just running. The sound of his grandfather's voice was all he needed to make him run. Run for his life. Run for the safety of the pickup.

When they reached the truck, Tom flung open the door. They all piled in, one after the other. And when they were inside, they locked the doors. They sat there, panting and trying to catch their breath.

"What is it, Grampa?" Dad puffed.

Tom was trembling. No matter how hard he tried, he couldn't make himself stop. Beside him, he could feel Grampa trembling, too—trembling and gasping for air.

It took some time before Grampa was breathing right again. When he finally caught his breath, he looked at Dad and pointed to where Sally and her calf were lying dead.

"Panther!"

He coughed. Then he said it again: "Panther."

The word left a chill in the air. A silence.

It was a long time before Dad could speak. "Did you see it?"

Grampa shook his head. "No. But it was there." He had to stop and breathe deeply for a while to get

his wind back. "Took me some time. But I remembered. I remembered seeing those tracks before. Long,
long time ago. They're cat tracks, all right. Panther.
Made its kill less than an hour ago. It's still around
some place. I can feel it."

Tom shuddered. He could hear Dad swallow.

"Are you sure? It could have been coyotes. Are
you sure it was a panther?"

Grampa's hand was shaking so much he couldn't
even light his pipe.

"I'm positive. You know better than that, Charlie.
Coyotes might drag down a newborn calf, but they
won't take on a cow. Not even when she's down.
Besides, you saw the tracks. It was a panther, all right.
And a big one at that."

"What do we do about it?" Dad wiped the sweat
from his forehead.

Grampa shook his head. "Best go back home and
get our guns." He glanced at the sun. "Got about
four hours of light left. But I doubt we'll ever find it.
You don't ever see a panther. Not unless they want
you to."

"We'll try it anyway." Dad started the pickup. "We
can't just let that cat kill our stock. Maybe we can get
a shot."

"Maybe," Grampa said. Only he didn't sound much
like he believed it.

Back at the house, no amount of pleading or begging or crying did any good. Dad just looked Tom square in the eye and said: *"No!"*

"But Dad, I'll stay close. I'll stay right beside you."

"I said no. You're not going with us. That's all there is to it. You stay here in the house with your mom and Susan."

"Oh, Dad," Tom moaned. "I'm not a baby. Why can't I go? Please?"

Dad didn't answer. He just looked at Tom real mean-like. There wasn't anything for him to do but sit down at the kitchen table and shut up.

Dad and Grampa got their rifles and left. It was just about the worst thing that could happen—Dad and Grampa going off hunting a panther and Tom having to stay behind with the women. He felt like a sissy, having to stay there at the house with all the excitement going on outside.

But there was no way around it. He couldn't do anything now, except sit around and wait with Mama and Susan. Wait and wonder what Dad and Grampa were doing, and worry about what might be happening out there.

10

One thing about being left behind—it's a lot better when somebody else is left behind with you. Two weeks after the panther killed Sally and her calf, Tom had all the company he needed. Justin arrived and so did a whole bunch of people from farms in the area. It seemed like Tom's house was filled with people.

The panther had been up to a lot of meanness since it had killed Sally and the calf. Two days later it got one of the Johnsons' calves. The snow melted and the cat disappeared with it. Then an ice storm hit and when the ice came, so did the cat. It killed Leonard Hall's best quarter horse mare. Three days later, it struck on the other side of the peak, chewing up one of Carl Garrison's show steers and leaving it to die.

The menfolk from the nearby ranches had gotten together at the Burkes' house for a hunt. A man by the name of "Fuzzy" Whitson brought his pack of trail hounds. At sunup the men left on horseback. They said they were going to take the dogs to where the cat made its last kill and see if they could sniff out its trail.

"The Game Rangers from the Wildlife Refuge are using helicopters and tranquilizer guns," Fuzzy said. "They'll never see that cat from the air. My hounds'll find him, though."

After the men left, Tom tried to count all the people in the house. But there were so many of them, he never did get them all counted. Everybody was chattering and laughing. Some of the women were in the kitchen helping Mama fix up a big feed for when the men came back. Some were visiting in the living room. It was like a big party instead of the serious business of hunting a panther. Everybody seemed happy and excited about it—everybody except Grampa.

Grampa was mad as a smoked hornet. Since the men were going on horseback and since the ice was still thick on the ground, they decided to leave Grampa behind.

"This ice being so slippery," Dad had said, "be awful easy for you to break them old bones. You best stay here."

Grampa took to that like a cat takes to being thrown

into a bathtub of cold water. To say he didn't like it wouldn't come anywhere close to describing how Grampa felt. He let out a string of words that made Mama cover up her ears and Tom's face turn plum red. And when he finished yelling he grabbed his coat and pipe and stormed off to the barn, muttering to himself all the way.

Mama had told Tom to go around and say hi to everybody. But when he got tired of thanking people for coming, he got Justin and they lit out for the barn too.

The sled was by the barn door, and they took turns pulling each other around the barnyard until their hands got cold. Then they went to look for Grampa.

When they found him in the workroom, Grampa didn't even look up. He was whittling on a stick and puffing his pipe.

"Mr. Burke," Justin asked, "may we talk to you awhile?"

Grampa nodded. "Might as well. What do you want to talk about?"

"Well, sir . . . we were wondering about the cat. You reckon they'll catch it?"

Grampa shook his head. "Nope."

Justin sort of frowned. "Well, Mr. Burke, you think they'll get close enough to get a shot at it?"

"Nope."

"You think they'll see it, sir?"

"Nope."

Justin rolled his eyes at Tom, then he walked around and sat beside Grampa. He pulled out a pocketknife and started whittling, too.

"How come you don't think they'll see it, Mr. Burke?"

Grampa put his knife aside. "They could have a whole army and a dozen packs of hounds. Still wouldn't get within a mile of that cat. Panther's stickin' to high ground, up in them hills where he can see everything that goes on. 'Sides that, there's fifteen horses and riders going helter-skelter, following a pack of noisy hounds. Even a cat that's half deaf could hear all the racket they're making. Probably heard them when they left the house. And as soon as he heard them, he doubled back on his track, then went to higher ground to hold up in some hard-to-get-at hiding place. Even a dumb cat would know to get moving with all that racket going on. And this one here ain't no dumb cat. Fact is, he's probably smarter than most."

"What makes you think he's so smart?" Tom asked.

Grampa smiled.

"'Cause he's here."

"What do you mean?" Justin frowned.

"Hard telling where that cat come from," Grampa said. "But these parts have been cleared out of panthers

for a long time. More people moving in all around—
and the more people, the farther back in the mountains
and brush they push the panthers. That means this one
probably came from the south range of the Rocky
Mountains. New Mexico more than likely.

"From here, that's around seven hundred miles.
Panther has to be mighty tough and powerful smart to
get that distance without somebody getting him.

"Bad winter like this probably drove him down from
the high mountains. Snow is always a lot worse in the
mountains than it is way out here. His food supply
run short on him, so he had to start moving south,
farther away from his hiding places and into the flat
lands. Couldn't find any deer in the mountains, so he
came into the flats and started feeding on cattle instead."

"Could he have been here since summer?" Tom
asked.

Justin nudged him with an elbow and shot him a real
dirty look. "You promised not to tell," he whispered.

Tom leaned close to his ear. "I didn't tell," he
whispered back.

Grampa didn't hear the commotion. "Hard telling
how long that cat's been around here," he answered.
"Could have been living up in the Wichitas and feeding
on deer and rabbit. But with this cold winter, if his
natural food supply run out . . . well . . ."

Justin scooted to the edge of the workbench.

"Do they eat people?"

Grampa shook his head. "No." Then a frown took hold of his face. He scratched at his chin. "'Course, they don't seem to be born with the natural fear of man like the common mountain lion is. That does make them awful dangerous. . . ."

Tom shuddered. He thought about his dad and the other men.

"You don't think it could get one of the men? It wouldn't kill anybody . . . would it?"

Grampa smiled.

"Not with 'em riding in a group like that. Like I said, that old cat's a smart one. He's done seen them riders coming. They won't get near him."

As usual, Grampa was right. Just about sundown, the men came riding back to the house. And from the first look at them, it was plain they hadn't seen the cat.

They were tired and cold, riding slow and all slumped over. There wasn't any talking or laughing. Tom knew if they'd shot the panther, they would have been whooping it up.

The women had a good supper fixed. The men ate quietly and didn't even talk much afterward while they were drinking their coffee. It was nearly midnight before everybody finally cleared out.

Tom stopped by Grampa's room on his way to bed.

"Grampa?"

"Yes, Tom."

"You reckon that panther will be back?"

Grampa pulled his nightshirt on over his head and thought for a long time before he answered.

"Hard to tell. With all them riders and hounds and helicopters out today, they might have spooked him clean out of the country. Or . . . could be up there on the peak, holed up in a cave or pile of rocks—just waiting. Hard telling what a panther will do, or where he will show up next."

11

Two weeks after the riders and the hounds had gone out, the panther still hadn't shown. Nobody had lost one calf, or one hog, or one single horse.

All the neighbors held their breath and watched their stock real close. But after two weeks and not one sign of the panther, most folks figured he had lit out for a new place where there weren't so many people. They figured their panther trouble was over.

In those two weeks, the ice melted and the weather warmed up a mite. Tom was glad about the warm weather. Only trouble was that when the warm weather came, Dad had to take off early of a morning on the tractor to work the fields, and that meant Tom had to go back to helping Grampa with the morning milking.

One morning, when they were milking, Tom asked, "Grampa, is Ginger really gonna have her a baby?"

Grampa didn't look up. "Yep," he answered.

"Then how come she ain't had it? You said it would be the last of February or early March."

Grampa cleared his throat. "Just nature's way. Besides, it's only the second week of March. That's still early."

Tom frowned. "Grampa, how come when you don't know the answer to something I ask, you always say, 'Just nature's way'?"

Grampa took the bucket of milk from under the cow he was milking and turned her into the lot. Tom finished his cow and followed him. They emptied the buckets and rinsed them out, then hung them upside down on wooden pegs so they'd be ready for the afternoon milking.

Grampa started poking around in his overalls, trying to find where he'd put his pipe and tobacco.

"How come you always answer like that?" Tom repeated.

Grampa scowled at him out of one eye. "One reason is that I don't rightly know. Another reason is what I do know, I don't know how to explain to you." Then he went to hunting for his pipe again.

"Try," Tom said.

Grampa glanced at him.

"Try what?"

"Try making me understand why Ginger ain't had her foal."

Grampa cleared his throat. He found his pipe, but he didn't light it. Instead, he turned to Tom and sort of threw up his hands.

"All right," he said. "You're gonna keep pestering me until I answer you, so I might as well try. When I told you Ginger's foal was gonna be here the end of February, I thought it was. But animals are different. And all this cold weather we been havin' makes a difference too. There ain't no way of knowin' for sure when a mare's gonna have her foal. Some just take longer than others. Seein's how this is Ginger's first foal, chances are it will be late.

"Cold winter might make the foal late, too. The only way I can explain *that* is that it's nature's way. How and why it works that way, I got no idea."

It sounded like a good, honest answer to Tom. He liked it when Grampa came right out and told him he didn't know why or how. That was a lot better than storying to him.

"You reckon Mrs. Riley would know, Grampa?"

Grampa shrugged. "Don't imagine she would. But . . . wouldn't hurt to ask her, I reckon."

Tom smiled and nodded his head. "I'll do that," he said. "First thing when I get to school."

"That reminds me." Grampa pulled his silver watch out of his overalls pocket and held it close to his face. "You don't get a move on, you ain't gonna make it. That old yeller bus gonna be here pretty quick, and you ain't even changed out of your milking clothes yet." He waved his hands like he was shooing flies. "You get on to the house. I'll finish up feeding the cows."

Tom headed across the lot. The early morning was a pretty time of day, he decided as he looked around him. Mighty pretty.

It was that time of day between the dark and the light—the time when the sun was just peaking over the top of the earth in the eastern sky. He paused a second, admiring the beautiful colors.

It gave Tom a good feeling, but when he got to the house, the good feeling left him. Dad's tractor was by the back door. He paused and listened.

There were usually sounds from the kitchen—Mama and Susan talking or the sound of pans rattling from Mama's cooking. And there was always the smell of bacon coming crisp and sharp to his nose when he opened the back door.

Only, this morning was different. There was no smell coming from the stove. There was silence where there should have been noise. The warm, busy feeling of early morning wasn't there, either.

Tom could tell something was wrong, even before he got into the kitchen.

Once inside the house, he knew something had happened. The gas burner was going on the stove, but nothing was cooking. There was a skillet of half-fried bacon on the counter. He touched it and found it was cold.

"Mama!"

When he called, there was no answer. Tom held his breath and listened.

"Dad?"

Still nothing.

Tom started to run back to the barn to get Grampa. But he stopped himself. He couldn't leave until he found out where everybody was.

There was a sound—a voice, calling to him. Upstairs. He ran up the steps, two at a time.

"Mama? Dad?"

"We're up here, Tom," his father called.

Dad met him at the top of the stairs.

"What's wrong?" Tom gulped. "Why ain't you and Mama in the kitchen? Where you been?"

His father put a finger to his lips. "Hush, boy. Keep your voice down. Your sister's bad sick."

Tom looked around him. The door to Susan's room was open. He could hear her voice from inside— moaning, crying.

"What's wrong? Is she hurt?"

Tom started to go around Dad to Susan's room, but Dad grabbed his arm.

"No, Tom. We don't know that what she's got ain't catchin'. You best not go in."

"But . . . Dad . . . if she's sick . . . I ought to see her. I want to see her."

"No. Now, listen. Mama and me are gonna take her into Lawton to the doctor. And I want you to do something for me."

He reached in his pocket and pulled out his keys.

"You take the keys to the truck and go downstairs. Make sure it's in neutral and start it. Then turn the heater on. Soon as it gets warmed up good, you come back up here and let us know."

Tom nodded. He took the keys and ran down the stairs. Grampa was just coming in the door as he raced out. Tom didn't even stop.

"It's Susan," he yelled. "She's sick. Up in her room."

He raced to the pickup and jumped in. The steering wheel was cold as ice in his hands. He'd started the pickup for Dad before. It was usually a big deal. It made him feel real important and grown up.

But this morning, he didn't even think about it. He just started it. He made sure the heater was running, and wished it would hurry and get warm.

He kept looking back to the house, worrying about Susan and wondering what was wrong with her. He prayed that she'd be all right.

Even though Susan was bossy and mean sometimes, she was still his sister. And now that she was sick, he started thinking about all the times she played with him and was nice to him. He remembered how she'd caught him fooling with Grampa's shotgun that day, and how she never told on him; and when he was grounded, she'd played checkers with him; and there was that night in the spring when a thunderstorm blew up and she'd come into his room and talked with him until he fell asleep.

Tom stuck his hand over the heater. The cold air was still blowing.

"Hurry," he growled. "Hurry and get warm, you darned old truck!"

He shuddered when he thought about all the times he'd sassed Susan. Right now, he wished he'd never stuck his tongue out at her or called her tattletale or pestered her when she was on the telephone with her new boyfriends. He wished he hadn't ever done any of those things.

He put his hands together in his lap and closed his eyes.

"Please, dear Lord . . . please let Susan be all right. Don't let nothin' happen to her. I promise I'll be nice to her. Oh, please, God . . . don't let her be too sick. Please don't let her . . ."

He felt the warm air on his face. His eyes flashed open. He put his hands down by the heater and felt the hot air blowing through his fingers.

In half a second, Tom was out of the pickup. He stomped on the emergency brake, like he'd seen Dad do, to make sure the truck wouldn't roll, then he ran to the house. He ran faster than he had ever run before.

The family was in the kitchen. Dad was carrying Susan in his arms. They had her wrapped up in blankets. All you could see were her face and her long red hair, falling rumpled and tangled over Dad's arm. She was white as a ghost. Her mouth was open and her eyes seemed like they were sunk way back in her head.

Dad's cheeks turned red from the strain of holding her. Even though she wasn't trying to, she made his job mighty tiresome. She kept wiggling around, grabbing her stomach, groaning and trying to double up in a knot. Dad shifted her in his arms. His eyes grew wide.

"Pickup warm?"

Tom nodded.

"Yes, sir. What's wrong, Dad? Is she gonna be all right?"

Dad didn't answer. He started for the door.

"Open the door, Tom. Amanda," he called to Mama. "Bring the stuff. Hurry."

Tom got behind the door and pulled it open wide. Dad rushed out with Grampa right on his heels. Mama followed with an overnight bag and some other stuff.

Tom started to go after them. Then, deciding he'd only be in the way, he waited there beside the door.

He could see Dad saying something to Grampa. Then they got in the truck and drove off. The mud spattered high as they sped away. Grampa stood watching in the middle of the barnyard. He waited until he could hear the engine winding out on the dirt road a quarter of a mile away. And when the sound of the truck stopped coming through the clear morning air, Grampa came back to the house.

"What is it, Grampa? What's Susan got? Is she gonna be all right?"

Grampa walked before him and into the kitchen. He carried his head low and his shoulders slumped.

"We don't know what's wrong with her, Tom. Don't know what she's got. Your dad said he'd call from the hospital, soon as they find out anything."

Tom looked out the door, in the direction the pickup had gone. He bit at his finger.

"Is there anything we can do. Grampa? Can't we help her?"

Grampa shook his head. "Only thing we can do is

wait. Wait and . . ." He looked up toward the ceiling and closed his eyes. "Wait and pray."

That's just what they did. They both sat quiet for a spell, praying for Susan to get better.

After a time, Grampa got up and fixed breakfast. But neither one of them ate very much. Tom helped him do the dishes, then they went in the living room and sat down near the table where the telephone was. They stared at it and waited.

The longer they waited, the harder the waiting got.

12

At six that evening, they were still perched on the edge of their chairs, staring at the telephone. A few times, Grampa had picked it up just long enough to check if it was working. Then he'd set it down and gone back to his chair.

Tom had a bad habit of biting his fingernails when he was nervous. Three of his nails were bleeding around the edges, where he had torn the nails down to the quick.

"Want some dinner, boy?" Grampa asked.

Tom shook his head.

"Aren't they ever gonna call, Grampa? Why don't they call?"

"They will, Tom. They'll call."

Only, it seemed like they never would. It seemed like that telephone never would ring.

Then it rang.

They both sprang to their feet. Grampa rushed to the phone. He picked it up and put it to his ear before the first ring was through.

"Yes?"

There was a silence. Grampa was holding his breath. Suddenly, his chest seemed to drop. All the air came rushing out. He turned to Tom.

"It's Justin. Tell him you can't talk long. Hurry and hang up."

Tom gritted his teeth together. Why did it have to be Justin? Why couldn't it be Mama or Dad? He took the phone from Grampa.

"Hello," he snapped.

"Hi, Tom. This is Justin. What ya doing? How come you weren't in school today?"

Tom bit his lip.

"It's Susan," he answered. "She come down bad sick this morning. Mama and Dad are supposed to call from the hospital. I got to hang up."

"Wait," Justin called. "Call me back when you find out about her, okay?"

"Okay. Goodbye."

" 'Bye."

He turned to Grampa.

"Justin wanted to know why I wasn't in school. I told him I'd let him know how Susan was."

Grampa nodded. He started to say something, but before the words came out, the phone rang again.

They both stood stock-still, looking at it. When it rang the second time, Grampa snatched it up.

"Hello? Yes?"

He listened, nodding his head from time to time. Tom could tell by watching him that it was either Mama or Dad on the phone. He couldn't tell what they were talking about, though.

Then Grampa smiled. He breathed a sigh of relief. And when he did, Tom could tell that Susan was okay.

He talked a while longer before hanging up.

"Your sister's gonna be all right." Grampa grinned. "She's gonna be fine."

"What was wrong?" Tom asked. "Why was she so sick?"

They went into the kitchen and Grampa answered while he fixed supper.

"Said her appendix broke."

Tom frowned, not knowing what that meant.

"It's a thing inside of you, near your stomach," Grampa explained. "Sometimes it swells up and makes you real sick. They had to operate on her, and Mama said they waited until they were sure she was in good shape before they called.

"I talked to your dad, and he said she was still asleep but she was doing fine. Said he and Mama were gonna stay at the hospital tonight so they could be with her. He said he listened to the weather report while they were in the waiting room and that there's another cold spell coming our direction. Wants us to get the milking done early tomorrow and stay in the house the rest of the day. He and your mother will probably be home by afternoon milking."

Tom felt his eyebrows raise up. "That mean I don't have to go to school tomorrow?"

Grampa shrugged.

"Can't do the milking and stay in the house if you're off at school. Guess missin' a couple of days won't hurt you too bad. We'll call Mrs. Riley after chores and see what your homework is."

Grampa laughed out loud then and slapped Tom on the back.

"Important thing is Susan's gonna be good as new. Has to stay there a few days, but she's gonna be all right."

"I sure am glad, Grampa."

"Me, too."

After they ate supper, Tom remembered he was supposed to call Justin back. He picked up the phone and dialed.

The phone rang at the other end of the line. Justin answered. "Hello?"

"Justin, this is Tom. Mama called. They said Susan is doing fine. Everything's all right."

"Good," Justin said. "When I told my mom and dad she was sick, they decided they'd go in to the hospital and see if there was anything they could do. They just left a few minutes ago."

Tom leaned back in his chair. He was relaxed now. He propped his feet up on the telephone table.

"Why did you call a while ago?" he asked.

Justin sighed. "Ah, I just wanted to tell you that our fishing trip was off for Saturday. Dad wants to go up to the panhandle to see his brother and he's taking us with him. We're supposed to leave Saturday morning."

"You gonna stay Sunday, too?" Tom asked.

"Probably. We'll start back late Sunday evening. You gonna be at school tomorrow?"

Even though Justin couldn't see him over the phone, Tom shook his head. "No. Dad called and said it's supposed to turn cold tomorrow and there're lots of chores to help Grampa with. Guess I'll stay home Friday."

"Well, I'll see you at school on Monday," Justin said. "My dad listened to the weather on TV, too. If the weather gets too bad, we'll probably miss out on going to the panhandle and going fishing both. Say, I got to go. My mom told me to get the dishes done and my room cleaned up before they get back from Lawton. I'm glad your sister's okay. See you Monday."

"See ya, Justin. 'Bye."

Grampa had already finished feeding the stock when Tom got off the phone. He went to the milk barn to help out there. Everything went fine until the old Jersey cow named Helen kicked at him and turned over a whole bucket of milk. It went all over the place, but most of it sloshed on Tom.

"Darn old cow," he yelled at her.

Helen only switched her tail and wiggled her ears. Tom turned her into the lot and started milking the last cow.

"Seems like all I'm good for around here is milking," he muttered. "Don't get to go to the hospital. Don't get to go fishing with Justin. Milking! That's all I ever do."

13

The next morning, it was the same thing—milking again.

It seemed warmer than it had been the last few weeks. That made the milking a little easier. There was a thick fog, though, the real heavy kind that swirled as you walked through it. It made it hard to see. When Tom got through milking and looked out the door toward the house, he could hardly see the lights in the kitchen.

He called for Grampa to come and look.

"It's a thick one, all right," Grampa said as he lit his pipe. "Lots of moisture in the air. Hope your mom and dad can see well enough to drive home."

Tom unbuttoned his coat and fanned his face with his hand.

"You reckon it'll stay warm like this until spring, Grampa?"

"Reckon not. We'll have us another cold spell. Almost bet money on it. Fact, it wouldn't surprise me if we had us a cold snap today."

Tom frowned. "What makes you think that, Grampa? How do you know it's gonna get cold?"

Grampa laughed. "Feel it in my bones, son. Old arthritis gets to acting up on me, I know there's a change in the weather coming." He groaned and rubbed at his shoulder. "Rheumatism is acting up, too."

He motioned Tom back into the barn.

"Now, come on. Let's get these cows fed so we can go eat breakfast. I'm starved."

"Me, too, Grampa!"

Tom scurried up to the loft and threw down some hay. They took turns carrying it to the trough where the cows ate. Then, while Tom was spreading it out, Grampa went back inside for some grain.

Tom whistled to himself while he worked. Then he stopped to catch his breath—and he heard it.

There was a stillness. A dead silence in the air. There wasn't a sound from anything, just the quiet.

The cows stood still. They weren't chewing their

hay. Not mooing. Not even breathing. They had their heads turned toward the south end of the lot, listening with their ears pointed high. They were standing like they were stone frozen in their tracks.

The fog was so thick, Tom couldn't see past the wood corral fence. But there was something there. He could feel it. Like that day at Skeeter Hole.

All of a sudden, the cows started mooing and bellowing. Moving and running around in front of the feed trough. Bawling and bumping into each other. All the time watching something—something out there beyond the fog. Something that scared them.

"What's going on?" Grampa called from the edge of the barn. "What's spookin' them cows?"

The cows bunched themselves up together. Then, just as quick as they had started their bawling and running around, they stopped. They stood stock-still.

Tom looked where they were looking. He squinted his eyes, strained to see.

There was nothing but the rolling fog and the silence.

Then he saw it. A form. A shape. Moving near the corral fence.

Through the fog, it was fuzzy, hard to make out.

It came closer. Right up to the fence at the far end of the lot. There, it stopped. It paused a second, then sprang. It jumped right up on the top rail, with no trouble at all. And when it landed it was as quiet as the fog itself.

It moved along the rail on sleek, noiseless feet. The big, black body took shape as it moved nearer. Tom saw the square head, the yellow-green eyes that pierced straight through the darkness of the fog—eyes that seemed to cut right down inside him.

Eyes he'd seen before. That thing he'd seen at Skeeter Hole.

Only this time it wasn't just the head or the eyes he saw. This time, he saw all of it—the sleek, muscular shoulders, the long body that rippled as it moved, the long tail.

He saw it, and he knew what it was.

"The panther!"

The words came loud and shrill through the still air. "Grampa!" Tom screamed. "It's the panther!"

The cat stopped. Glared at Tom with those tight, yellow-green eyes. Watched him like it was watching its very next meal.

There was the loud clattering sound of metal pails banging together inside the barn. Then Grampa was screaming and yelling.

The cat took one last look at Tom before one mighty spring carried it from the rail, back into the fog. It was gone, like it had vanished from the face of the earth. All that was left was the gray fog, swirling and silent.

Grampa came from the barn. He had the long pitchfork tucked under his arm. In his hands, he carried two milk pails, banging them together as hard as he could. Tom jumped from the feed trough and ran to him.

"I saw it, Grampa. I saw the panther. He was right there. On the fence. He was coming after me."

Grampa dropped the buckets and pitchfork. He swooped Tom up against him.

Tom buried his face in Grampa's chest. He was shaking so hard he couldn't stop. Grampa held him tight, patting his back.

"It's all right, boy. He's gone. Noise scared him off. We're all right."

Grampa helped him to the house.

Even being safe inside, Tom couldn't stop shaking. He sat huddled against the kitchen stove. It was like that cat was coming after him—not the cows or anything else, but Tom. And when he thought about how close that panther had come and the way its eyes glowed when it saw him, he couldn't stop the trembling.

Grampa kept telling him that the panther wouldn't be back. He got the checkerboard out of the cabinet and talked Tom into a couple of games. Like usual, Grampa won both of them. It *did* help take Tom's mind off the panther, though. Neither one of them felt like eating breakfast, but around ten or so, Grampa fixed them some sandwiches. They went to the living room and turned on the TV while they ate. Grampa stretched out on the couch when he finished eating. Tom sat in the big chair, but he couldn't get comfortable. Every time a commercial came on, he'd get up and go look out the window.

It was scary, looking into the fog. But around one o'clock, the fog started to clear. Tom could see for a long ways, and the panther wasn't anyplace around.

At last Tom curled up in the big chair. Grampa had fallen asleep watching TV, and his snoring from the couch made Tom feel sleepy, too. He closed his eyes. The chair felt warm and soft. And in no time at all, he was asleep.

14

There was a coughing sound. Tom blinked his eyes. The sound came again. It was Grampa. Tom forced his eyes open.

"Good gosh, it's cold in here." Grampa coughed. "Wonder what's going on."

Even though he'd been asleep, Tom had tucked himself up in a little ball in the chair and pulled the cushion down over him. It took some struggling to get untangled. But when he did, he followed Grampa to the window.

The wind was rattling the glass. They could feel the cold puffing in around the edge.

"Looks like that cold front's hit," Grampa said. "Best get us a fire started. Come on."

They went to the woodpile beside the house and

started dragging in wood. The wind bit at them the second they walked out the door. Tom could feel his ears and cheeks hurting from the cold. The pieces of blackjack logs in his hands were like ice chunks from the horse trough. By the time they got inside with the first load of wood, his teeth were clacking together like a woodpecker pounding on a tree.

Grampa couldn't seem to shake his cough. It was a growling sort of sound. He was coughing and hacking like there was a bucket full of gravel rattling around in his throat.

"Musta caught me a chill," he said, rubbing his hands together. "Tom, you get some kindling and I'll stay here—see if I can get this old fire going."

Tom started for the door.

"Put your coat and gloves on, boy," Grampa called.

Outside, the sky was a dark gray color. Big, ugly clouds banked up in the north. If it had been spring or summer, Tom would have figured them for thunder banks—the kind that brought hail and heavy winds and even tornadoes. But in the winter, he didn't know what to make of them. Whatever was in those clouds, it sure made them look mean.

Carefully, Tom picked out some kindling and medium-sized pieces of wood from near the bottom of the woodpile.

That would be enough for Grampa to get the fire

started. After taking the wood inside, Tom came out again and got three good logs. He picked big round ones, the kind that would burn slowest and make the best coals.

While he was hunting the logs, something started falling from the clouds. He could hear it pattering on the ground. Every once in a while, he felt a sharp, cold sting against his face. Little chunks of ice hit the woodpile. They bounced, then scattered like marbles rolling over hard sand.

It seemed like no time at all until the fine, driving sleet was everywhere. It covered the ground and the woodpile. Even a thin film had started to freeze on the three logs he was holding in his arms.

Tom scurried for the house.

Grampa was kneeling by the fireplace. He already had some crumpled-up paper burning and was adding the small sticks of kindling to it. The flames lapped at the wood. They crackled, turning yellow and blue as they struggled to catch.

"Two secrets to starting a fire," Grampa said, without taking his eyes from his work. "First off, got to put the kindling and small stuff on the bottom. Second, you got to spread it some, so it can get plenty of air."

He fanned the small flames with his hand. Then he took a deep breath and blew gently. The fire popped and crackled. It grew until it was burning just right.

"See?" Grampa smiled.

Tom nodded. "I'll go after some more logs."

Grampa got to his feet. "No. This will do until we get back. Besides, I don't want you out there alone."

Tom frowned. "Get back from where, Grampa?"

"The barn. We got to get the milking and chores done."

Tom bit his lip. "But Dad told us to stay inside. He said he'd be home for afternoon milking."

Grampa's coat was lying on the back of the couch. He started putting it on.

"That was before this sleet storm hit. Your dad wasn't figuring on all this ice when he told us to stay inside. Chances are, the roads are already slick. He and your mom will be awful late comin' back from the hospital. We don't get them cows milked right now, it'll be too dang cold and too dang late to do it when he gets home. Come on."

Tom hesitated. "But Grampa..." he stuttered. "What if... if the... what if the panther is out there?"

Grampa chuckled. "After all the noise this morning, that cat's long gone. He's probably up on Panther Peak hid out in some cave, trying to keep warm." He stuck his pipe in his mouth. "Now, let's get our work done so we can get back in where it's warm."

Before going outside, Grampa went upstairs and got his shotgun. Knowing he had it, Tom felt a lot safer.

The wind was howling something terrible. It drove the sharp, icy pellets against the side of Tom's face. Even when he ducked his head against the wind, it still drove against his hair, hard enough so he could feel the sting.

By the time they got to the barn, they were both covered with ice. It was real cold, and when it hit their warm clothes, the stuff stuck to them like cockleburs sticking to a cow's tail. Inside the barn, they brushed each other with their hands. They used their fingernails to pull the ice out of their hair.

"I seen it coming down when I watched you fetch the wood," Grampa said. "But I had no idea it was coming down this hard. Wouldn't surprise me if your mom and dad had to stay in Lawton tonight. This is a rough one. It's a regular blizzard!"

The cows had calmed down a lot since the morning. Just by the way they were acting, Tom could tell his grandfather was right—the panther was no place around.

Helen was the last cow into the milking stalls. Grampa was already emptying the other pails of milk into the cooler when Tom brought her in.

He scooted his stool up and reached out to start milking. Then, remembering how feisty she'd been lately, he stopped.

"Reckon we ought to put the kickers on old Helen?" he called. "She's been awful touchy."

"Wait a minute," Grampa called from the back of the barn.

In a little bit, he came back with a pail of feed. He set it down in front of her, then walked around to where Tom was.

"That old cow's a bit ornery. Still, there's no call for her to be kicking at ya all the time." He motioned to get up. "Here, I best take a look at her."

Grampa was careful about watching her hooves. Being sure he could dodge if she kicked, he started feeling under her. After a minute he turned to Tom, smiling.

"I figured there was a reason for her acting so mean. She's got a cut on her milk bag. Musta straddled some barbed wire. Go. get me that medicine in the blue bottle, Tom."

Tom hurried to the cabinet in the milk room where they kept the medicine and stuff for the cows. He got the bottle down and took it back to Grampa.

"Here."

"This ought to fix her up," Grampa said.

He took the bottle and opened it. Then he got the dauber out and leaned over.

Just as he was starting to doctor the cut, his pipe

slipped from his overalls. He saw it. And just as he touched the blue medicine to Helen, he reached with the other hand to pick his pipe up.

Helen wiggled around, then jumped and kicked, faster than Tom could blink his eyes.

Her big hoof hit Grampa alongside the hip. It sent him spinning off the stool and across the barn.

"Grampa!" Tom screamed.

Grampa didn't answer. He was lying flat on his back. Tom ran to him and knelt down. Grampa's eyes were closed. His breathing was real light.

"Grampa?" Tom shook him. "Grampa, you all right? Grampa!"

Tom shook him again. Grampa didn't move. He just lay there. Tom felt the tears welling up in his eyes. But he fought them back. Grampa needed help. He couldn't take time to start crying, not now.

No amount of shaking or talking would wake Grampa up. It was like he was dead. Tom didn't know what to do.

Trembling all over, Tom ran to the barn door and looked out.

The sleet had turned to snow—a thick, driving snow that made it hard to see. Tom squinted. There was only the howl of the wind and the swirling sound of the snow.

Tom ran back to Grampa's side and knelt over him.

His face was white. Tom put his ear down against his chest. He could hear his heart pounding. When he put his cheek next to Grampa's nose, he could feel his breath. It came short and quick—like he was having trouble breathing.

"Oh, Grampa," he cried, "please don't be hurt bad. Please don't die. Oh, Grampa."

Tom had never felt so alone or so helpless. There was no one to run to. No one to tell him what to do. Tom was all by himself. Alone and scared.

15

It seemed like forever that he sat there and watched his grandfather.

At last, Grampa's eyes fluttered. He blinked, forcing them open. Tom grabbed him and laid his head on his chest.

"Oh, Grampa, you're alive. I was so scared."

Grampa said something, only Tom couldn't hear him. He sat up and leaned his ear close to Grampa's lips.

"What?"

Grampa's voice was barely a whisper. "I'm hurt bad, Tom. Think my hip's broke. Can you get me inside?"

Tom felt his eyes grow wide. He looked at Grampa.

"I . . . I don't know. I'll try."

It was hard for Grampa to smile, but he did.

"Good. Just try. I'll help all I can, Tom—only, the pain's pretty bad. I'm liable to pass out on you. If I do"—he coughed—"don't get scared, boy. If I pass out, just keep going. Don't stop. Don't leave me out there in the cold."

Tom nodded his head.

"Can you walk if I help?"

"No. You'll have to drag me."

Tom tried to take hold under Grampa's arms. He could barely move him. Grampa helped all he could. He tried scooting himself along with his hands.

It took Tom only a few minutes to know he could never make it to the house like this.

He looked around, trying to find something that might help him. There had to be some way to drag him through the thick snow that was falling outside.

The sled!

Tom saw it against the wall. Quickly, he got it and set it down next to Grampa. The big leather plow harness was hanging next to the feed bin.

That would work fine, he thought.

In a little while, he was all ready. With Grampa helping, they had managed to get him on the sled. Then Tom got some rope and tied him on, tight around his chest. If Grampa fell off outside, they might freeze before Tom could get him back on.

Tom put the harness around his chest and shoulders. It would be easier pulling with the harness than trying to pull a rope with his hands.

He leaned forward, straining to make sure it would hold the weight.

"Ready, Grampa?"

Grampa groaned.

Tom leaned into the harness with all his strength. He could feel his heart pounding in his head. The muscles in his legs and back were straining like they were fixing to pop.

Slowly, the sled started to move. An inch at a time.

Tom felt his legs churning. His feet were digging hard into the ground. The dirt on the barn floor made a grinding sound on the metal runners of the sled.

Then they were moving. Once outside, Tom had to be extra careful. The snow and ice were slippery under foot. If he fell, the runners on the sled might stick and he might not get it moving again.

The sled was easier to pull once it was in the snow. But Grampa's weight was still heavy. The going was hard.

The blizzard was swirling and blowing so thick Tom couldn't even see the house.

Just when he was about to give up, just when he figured he'd never make it and that his legs were too weak to carry him another inch, they were there.

The steps to the back porch were covered with snow. So Tom pulled the sled clean up onto the porch and inside the screen door.

The sled tore deep ruts into the tile of the kitchen floor, making squealing, squeaking sounds as Tom dragged it across.

With Grampa inside the house, Tom dropped the harness from around his shoulders. He staggered back to the door and closed it, blocking out the cold wind. Then, he came back to his grandfather's side.

Tom's head was swirling. He could feel himself weaving back and forth. Things were going round and round, like he was about to fall.

He collapsed on the floor beside his grandfather. He could hear his own heart pounding in his ears. Everything was wheeling and spinning. Then the world went black. He passed out.

Grampa's weak hand shaking his arm woke him. He struggled to his knees.

Grampa was still tied to the sled. He looked up at Tom and smiled weakly.

"You done it, Tom. I don't know how, but you done it."

His eyes fluttered. His head flopped to the side.

"Grampa?" Tom shook him. "Don't go to sleep. Please, Grampa. Don't leave me alone."

Grampa rolled his head back and looked up. "I'll try, Tom. I'll try to stay awake."

Just as soon as he said it, his eyes rolled back in his head. Tom shook him again.

"Tell me what to do, Grampa. Wake up! Grampa!!"

But his eyes were closed. He was asleep.

Tom looked at him a moment, then got to his feet. He ran to the other room and picked up the phone. With trembling fingers, he dialed 911.

Nothing happened! There was a humming sound over the phone. The emergency number didn't work. He put the receiver down, then picked it up and dialed 0.

"I'll tell the operator. She can send help."

The operator didn't answer. Tom clicked the little knobs up and down real fast. There was nothing but the humming sound. Then there was nothing at all. Just a silence.

The phone was dead.

Tom knew what had happened. The ice and snow had piled up on the lines some place and broken them. That phone was dead. Useless. He slammed it down and ran back to Grampa.

Tom knew he couldn't leave him lying on that sled. Straining and groaning, he dragged it into the living room, up close to the fire, and laid out some blankets and pillows on the floor next to it. Then he untied the ropes and moved Grampa over.

He seemed to rest comfortably there. His breathing got easier, and a little of the color came back to his face. Tom got some more wood and built the fire up.

But after a time, Grampa's red cheeks started turning white again. He was pale and sick-looking.

Tom knew there was just one thing left for him to do. No matter how scared he was, there was only one way he could get help for his grandfather.

He had to go after it. He had to walk to Justin's house. Justin's dad would know what to do.

16

"Tom. What are you doing?"

His grandfather's voice was soft as a whisper. Tom knelt beside him, trying to smile.

"You got to have help, Grampa. The phone's dead. I have to go get help for you."

Grampa grabbed his coat sleeve. "No, you can't!"

Tom tried to smile again. "I can make it. I got on plenty of heavy clothes. And I have gloves." He held them out. "I even found your shotgun."

He dragged it around so Grampa could see it.

"It's loaded. And I won't be scared, now that I got it."

Grampa shook his head again and again. "No, boy! You'll freeze to death. You can't go."

"I have to. Else you'll die. I have to go."

Grampa managed to prop himself up on one elbow. "You can't make it, Tom. You got to go by the lake road at the end of Skeeter Ridge. That wind and snow coming off that open lake will cut you in half. Even with warm clothes, you take to open ground—and you'll freeze, sure as I'm lying here."

Tom frowned. "I'll stick to the ridge, then. Stay in the creek bottom and cut through Panther Peak. I know a shortcut. I'll be out of the wind there."

Grampa fell back on the pillows.

"No, Tom. My gosh, no! The panther . . . remember. That's his ground. You can't go that way!"

Tom shuddered. "I can't just sit here and watch you die, Grampa."

Tom got to his feet. The big, double-barreled shotgun was heavy, but if he cradled it in his arms, he could carry it.

He'd never before done something his grandfather had told him not to. Only, this time was different. He knew if he didn't get help, Grampa would die. And with all this ice and snow, Mama and Dad were probably stuck in Lawton. If they knew something was wrong, they'd come home—no matter what. Only, they didn't know there was trouble.

"Tom!"

Grampa sat up, staring at him. His eyelids seemed

heavy, like he could barely keep them open. Tom looked back at him.

"Ginger," he breathed. "Take Ginger. Horseback is the only way you got a chance."

"But she's fixing to have her foal. Might have it anytime."

Grampa coughed. "She can still carry a rider. She can carry you right up to the time she has the foal. Listen to me, boy . . ." he made a wheezing sound in his throat when he breathed. "You saddle that horse and take her. Ride her hard. If you let her go slow, you'll freeze before you can get to Justin's."

Tom looked him straight in the eye and nodded. "I'll ride her," he promised.

Tom kept telling himself that the snow would let up, that any time now the wind would die down and things would start to clear.

But outside it was worse than ever. The snow looked like white bedsheets flopping in the breeze. One thick blanket of whirling, driving snow after another. The air was thick with it, and the ground was already covered.

Tom had to feel his way to the barn, leaning against the raging wind.

He knew it wasn't the snow that made traveling so dangerous—it was the Oklahoma wind. Inside the barn, he could not feel the cold at all. But outside, in the wind, it was a different story. It drove the snow like millions of tiny knives against him. It cut through the tiny holes in his clothing—the gaps between his gloves and his coat sleeves.

Ginger's saddle was hanging near her stall. Tom started to take it down; then, shaking his head, he decided to leave it. Ginger was warmer than a saddle. Riding her bareback, he would be closer to her.

He put the bit in her mouth. He had to stand on his tiptoes to secure the headstall over her ears.

"Come on, girl," he said coaxing her from the warm stall. "We got some riding to do."

Ginger moved slowly. Her sides bulged out so far with the foal she was carrying, she could barely fit through the stall door. Along with being big around, she was a tall horse, too. She was too tall for Tom to jump on her back, so he had to move her alongside the grain bin.

When he picked up the big shotgun and started to get on her back, she shied away. He climbed down and lead her in a circle, bringing her up to the bin once more.

She did fine until he picked up the shotgun. Then, her ears went to wiggling. Her eyes rolled around to look at it. And she stepped sideways—too far away for him to get on.

He had to climb down again and lead her back. This

time, though, he was ready for her. He stood there, on the bin but facing the other direction, with his back turned to her. He started humming to himself while he bent down to pick up the big gun. Out of the corner of his eye, he looked to make sure she was still standing next to the bin.

Then, all of a sudden, he turned and leaped for her back.

Ginger stepped sideways, but it was too late. Tom was already on her. He cradled the shotgun over the bend of his arms and took the reins in his hand.

"I know you don't want to," he said. "But I'm on you and we're goin'. So there!"

He turned her toward the door and kicked her gently in the sides. She started moving—only, she walked like she was on eggshells. She looked out the door at the snow and perked her ears at the raging wind. Then she stopped.

"Got to go fast. Make her move." Tom repeated the words his grandfather had said. "Else you'll freeze."

Tom nudged her with his heels.

She took one step, and that was all.

Tom ground his teeth together, glaring at her.

"I've had about enough of your foolishness," he growled, trying to make his voice sound mean—like Grampa did when he was mad at one of the cows. "We're going out there, whether you want to or not."

He took a firm hold on the reins, and brought his feet in hard against her sides, popping her with the reins at the same time.

They took out of the barn at a gallop—right into the mouth of the roaring storm.

They edged around the barn and turned west toward the ridge. Their backs were to the wind now. It made the traveling easier. Still, it was hard to see.

Tom made the mare stay at a fast gallop. It was open ground from the barn to the ridge. On the flat, the wind tore at them and whipped around their ears. They had to move when they were out in the open or else they'd end up like Grampa said—frozen to death.

It was hard hanging on to the heavy shotgun and slapping Ginger with the reins at the same time, but Tom managed. It was scary, running his horse full out into the blinding snow. Any second they might run on a small ravine or into a tree without seeing it until it was too late. Still, Tom kept the horse running, for the shelter of the ridge.

They made it to the creek. Ginger's sides were heaving in and out when they reached the base of Skeeter Ridge. Breathing was hard for her in the cold air—and in her condition. Tom's arms and legs were stiff. Inside his gloves, his fingers could barely move. He could not feel the reins in his hand.

The trees that lined the ridge loomed like misty shadows above them. Their bare limbs stretched out into the snow-filled sky like ghostly fingers reaching up for the warmth of a hidden sun.

As near as Tom could tell, it was about five o'clock. That left him a little less than an hour of daylight. If he didn't reach Justin's by dark, he would never reach it.

He kept pounding his heels into Ginger's shoulders, driving her on.

The trail at the base on the ridge was treacherous. Tom had to duck and dodge to avoid the trees with low-hanging branches. He clung close to Ginger's back, to keep from being scraped off. In places there were fallen limbs, half buried by the heavy snow. Ginger tripped, but each time she managed to catch herself.

As they neared the shortcut beneath Panther Peak, the wind and snow seemed to let up. Sheltered by the high ridge and the thick trees, they were below the icy hands of the wind. The trees blocked some of the snow and made the path easier to follow.

Then they were at the shortcut. Above them, even through the thick, whirling snow, Tom could see it— Panther Peak. Tall and ominous, it towered straight in front of them. It looked down like some angry giant.

Tom drew back on the reins and stopped. The place where they stood was familiar—a place he'd seen before, a place he remembered, a place that scared him.

He didn't know why—not at first. Then, a few feet away, he saw a pile of fallen brush. And beside it, a pile of cow bones, half covered by the snow.

This was the place where Sally and her calf had been killed by the panther. Tom remembered it now. And when he remembered, the air seemed to rush from his lungs. He couldn't move.

"Grampa needs help," he heard himself whisper. "He'll die if you don't bring help. Don't be scared. Go on. Go on!"

He sat up straight, squeezing his grandfather's shotgun tight in his hands.

"Let's go, Ginger," he called. "Come on."

But Ginger didn't move. She was panting and weaving from side to side beneath him. Tom kicked her with his heels.

Ginger heaved under him, breathing deeply. He kicked her again, but she wouldn't move.

Then, suddenly, her knees buckled. She went down under him.

The instant one of Tom's feet hit the ground, he threw himself to the side, managing to fall away from her. He rolled once as the snow piled thick around the neck of his coat. Then he was on his feet.

"Ginger!" he screamed. "Get up. Get up."

He grabbed the reins and pulled her. She wouldn't move. She just lay there, breathing hard, straining. Her side heaved in and out.

"She's not hurt," Tom told himself. "We were stopped when she fell—she couldn't have broken a leg. And we haven't gone far enough for her to be exhausted. We haven't run far enough to make her collapse."

"What's wrong, Ginger?" he yelled. "Get up. You've got to get up."

Then he knew what was wrong. He could see her sides tighten, then relax. He could see her bulging stomach strain and push.

Ginger was going to have her foal.

Tom fell to his knees at her side. "Oh, no," he begged. "Not now, Ginger. You can't have your foal now. You can't have it here."

His tears felt warm on his cold cheeks.

"Why? Why do you have to have your baby now?"

17

Tom knelt beside the newborn foal, holding its weak, wobbly head in his lap.

"Darn fool horse." He smiled. "You sure picked a heck of a time to get yourself born."

The foal blinked its eyes and struggled in his arms. Ginger was beside them. She started licking the foal, rubbing its wet hair with her tongue.

"You're right," Tom said. "We got to get this little girl dry, before she freezes."

He took off his stocking cap and started rubbing the foal with it—fast and hard, trying to dry the short, fine hair.

Ginger had wasted no time having her foal. Tom

had barely had time to drag up some dead limbs for a windbreak before it came. He'd put them in a U shape around where Ginger was lying. It blocked the cold wind. He built it high enough to keep the snow out. And, at times, when the wind let up, it seemed almost warm in the rugged shelter he'd made.

He hadn't had much choice about what to do. If he had left Ginger and gone on, the foal would have frozen to death. Being out in the storm like this, she couldn't live without his help. "Besides," he'd told himself, "it won't take too long. As soon as the foal's safe, I can go on. Get help for Grampa."

Ginger kept licking and Tom kept rubbing until the foal was dry. When Tom could feel her little heart pounding, pumping the warm blood to her fresh skin, he scooted away, leaving it beside her mother.

"Grampa says a foal's got to get to its feet before it's all right," Tom said. "Come on, little girl. Get up."

The foal raised her head weakly. She looked around, then, she kicked her feet. Struggling, she got to her knees. She tumbled back on her side and lay there a minute, breathing hard, before trying again.

The third time, she made it.

The foal stood beside her mother. Her legs were spread wide apart to keep her balance. Wobbly, spindly legs shook under her, but she was up.

"Go get some milk." Tom laughed. "You earned it."

He was sure the foal was safe now. Ginger would stay in the windbreak he had built for them. She would keep her foal warm and protected until someone could come for them. Tom got to his feet. He picked up the big shotgun and turned toward the ridge. It was time to go on.

He heard it, then—heard it for the first time. He had been so busy with the new foal, he hadn't noticed before. But when he stood up to leave, he heard it.

The silence.

The dead, lonely, frightening silence. And, as he froze, listening, he could sense it. He could feel it in his bones. Something watching. Eyes on him. Eyes that stared straight into him. Eyes that didn't blink, didn't move.

The panther was some place—watching him.

The storm had stopped. The wind didn't blow. The snow didn't fall.

There was only the empty silence—the white, empty stillness of the snow. And the panther, dark and evil. It lurked some place out there. Watching. Waiting. Moving on silent cat's feet—stalking its prey. Stalking Tom.

The shotgun was in his hands. He raised it, bracing himself against one of the dead limbs on top of the windbreak. Tom could almost feel the panther's breath through the cold chill of the air.

Wherever it was, Tom would be ready. There were two hammers on the shotgun, one for each barrel. Tom had to wrap both thumbs around one. He pulled back with all his might. Finally, it made the clicking sound that told him it was cocked.

Slowly, never taking his eyes from the rocks and trees around their shelter, he reached for the trigger.

Then it was there. The panther. Far off, near the ridge. He saw its form, slinking toward him. Like a shadow, it moved slowly. Careful. Coming closer. Closer.

There was a patch of white, glistening snow between the rocks and a large cottonwood tree. The cat came to the edge and stopped.

Tom could see it now. Before, it had been only a shape, a form—like he had seen it through the fog at the barn. Now it was clear.

The panther was huge. It was black as the night. Its muscles seemed to ripple as it crouched, moving slowly to the edge of the open ground. Even at this distance, Tom could see its eyes—the yellow-green that seemed to shine like candles against its black face.

Tom's heart was pounding in his ears. His breath caught in his throat. The cat came into full view on the open ground.

Tom squeezed the trigger. There was a roaring boom. The shotgun slammed back against his shoulder. A cloud of smoke belched form the barrel, blinding him from everything that was beyond.

The force rocked him backward. It sent him tumbling into the soft white snow. Ginger and the foal jumped with the sound of the shotgun. They moved away—but not far.

Tom struggled to his feet. He clawed his way back to the side of the windbreak. Looked over, staring with open eyes at where he had shot the panther.

The panther wasn't there.

There was no sign of it. There was only the white snow. The black shadow was gone. Tom could see where the blast from the shotgun had struck. He could see the places where the smooth snow was piled and busted away. But there was no panther.

His shot had missed.

Tom panicked. His hands trembled. His legs shook as if he were about to fall. He grabbed for the dead branches. Held himself there.

"Maybe he's gone," he told himself. "Maybe the shot scared him away."

But a feeling inside told him he was wrong. The panther was still out there. The roaring blast of the shotgun had scared it, but not enough to make it run away. It was still there. Still coming for Tom.

With both thumbs, he brought back the second hammer on the shotgun. "Why didn't I bring more shells?" he wondered. "Why only two? This is my last one. If I miss him with this one . . ."

The thought was too horrible. Tom held his eyes tight. He kept looking in all directions.

Something told him the cat would not show itself again, not until it was close enough to rush in and leap.

The foal was standing next to Ginger's side. Her fear made her wobbly legs shake even more than before.

"Poor little thing," Tom thought. "She's so weak she can barely stand."

Then it came to him. The panther wasn't after him at all. It was after the foal—the newborn baby. Weak and helpless—that was what the panther was after. That's what it had come for.

There was a big tree just a few feet away. One of the branches hung low, well within Tom's reach. "All I've got to do is get up there," he thought. "Climb clear to the top, where the panther can't reach. I'd be safe there, until the panther's gone."

He looked down at the big shotgun in his hands.

"To get up the tree, I'd have to leave the shotgun here. I'd have to leave Ginger and the foal," he thought.

He closed his eyes for a second. When he did, he could see Sally and her calf. He could remember how they looked that day he and Dad and Grampa had found them. He could still see how they looked after the panther had finished with them.

His finger went to the trigger of the shotgun. He held it firm against his side and braced his feet.

There was a sound. Snow crunched.

A movement caught his eyes.

He turned his head just in time to see it. The black shape leaped from behind the low, thick limbs of a cedar tree to his left. It raced through the glistening white powder toward him like a shadow on the snow.

He could hear its paws crunching the snow as it ran.

He could see its face, see its horrible, open mouth, see the white fangs, glistening against its open, snarling lips.

The shotgun was heavy. He jerked it against his shoulder.

The panther screamed—a shrill, piercing sound that sent the hair standing up on Tom's neck.

The shotgun swung in his hand.

The panther leaped—a snarling, black ball of fury aimed straight at Tom.

He squeezed the trigger.

There was a loud explosion and another terrifying scream from the cat.

Then it struck him. A claw ripped his shoulder. A

white fang from its open mouth tore the side of his cheek.

Tom screamed.

The force of the panther's leap knocked him backward. His head struck the ground. There was a cracking sound and everything went black.

18

A voice was calling out his name.

Tom opened his eyes, but he couldn't see. There was only blackness.

The voice came again, far off, like the sounds heard in a dream.

"Tom! Where are you? Tom!"

He tried to get up, but a heavy weight forced him down. He could feel the knot at the back of his head, pounding against his skull, throbbing. His face felt warm. Wet. He made his tongue trace around his lips. The strange, bitter taste of blood was in his mouth.

"Tom!" the voice came again, louder than before.

He was awake now. He still couldn't see. There was something heavy on his chest and head. He couldn't get up.

"Where are you, Tom?" The voice was close. Very close.

Tom opened his mouth. "Over here," he called. "Here. Help me!"

"Tom?"

"Help me," he called back. "Please."

Suddenly, the weight was being lifted from his chest. He blinked, forcing his eyes open.

Dad was standing above him. He picked him up and held him so he wouldn't fall. There were other men there. Tom could hear happy, excited voices—a lot of them.

Dad held him back at arm's length and looked at him.

"Thank heavens you're all right." Tears came to his father's eyes. "I don't know how . . . Oh, thank heavens . . ."

After a minute, Dad pointed to the ground beside them.

Tom was so weak, he could barely stand. Then one of the other men was beside him, helping his dad hold him up.

"Look," the man said.

There on the ground, at their feet, was the panther.

It was dead. There was a big hole right over its heart where the blast of the shotgun had hit him.

"How did you let it get so close?" one of the men asked. "That shot killed it straight off—but it must have been so close it landed on you."

"That panther was laying right on top of you when we come," another voice said. "Right on top of you!"

Tom felt dizzy. He felt his legs give way beneath him. He knew he was about to pass out.

"Grampa," he whispered. "Grampa's hurt."

Dad caught him.

"I know. He's all right. Mama's taken him to the hospital. He's gonna be all right."

There was more talking. Only, Tom couldn't hear it. Even though the men were right there beside him, they sounded far away. Muffled and faint.

Right before Tom passed out, he felt his dad pick him up in his arms. "You're gonna be all right, boy. You're safe."

Tom woke up, once, in the backseat of somebody's car. He dozed off, and when he awoke the second time, Mama was with him in a small room with bright lights and the smell of medicine heavy in the air. He could hear Dad answering a lot of questions about insurance and stuff like that.

When Tom woke up the third time, he was in the

hospital. He was lying on clean, crisp white sheets. The room was warm and comfortable.

There was a familiar smell in the room—the smell of Grampa's pipe. Tom opened his eyes. When he tried to sit up, a sharp pain in his shoulder knocked him back down, so he rolled to his other side and brought himself up with his good arm.

Grampa was lying in a hospital bed next to his. He was sitting up, smoking his pipe. When he saw Tom awake, he smiled.

"How you feelin', boy? That shoulder's a mite sore, I bet."

Tom looked at his shoulder. There was a pile of white bandages and tape over it. Grampa was sure right about it being sore. There was a bottle hanging on a stand by his bed and a tube running to his arm.

"What's that?"

"Antibiotics," Susan answered. "Keep you from getting an infection."

Mama and Dad and Susan were standing at the foot of his bed. Susan had on her robe and was stooped over, holding her stomach where she'd had her operation, but she was smiling when Tom looked at her. She looked healthy as a horse.

Tom shook his head, frowning. "Where am I? What happened?"

Mama sat on the edge of his bed. "You're in the

hospital," she said. "You're all right. You're gonna be fine."

Tom looked around. "Why? Why am I here?"

Dad came up and sat down on the other side of him. "Lost a lot of blood from where that panther clawed you. The doctors got you sewed up, right good. Said you'll be up and around in no time."

It hurt in his shoulder, but Tom managed to scoot up high enough in bed so he could see over to where Grampa was.

"Are you okay, Grampa?"

Grampa laughed. "Long as I got my pipe to smoke, I'm always fine." He pointed at the big cast that went from his waist clean down to his ankle. "Fool doctors got me wrapped up like a pig in a poke. Said I got a busted hip. Gonna keep me here a month or so." He shook his head. "Darned fools."

Tom looked up at his father. "Is Ginger and her foal . . . are they . . . alive?"

Dad nodded. "Both of 'em are fine. Healthiest little filly I ever seen. Got them in the corral back at the house."

Susan came up beside Tom. She leaned over the bed and kissed him on the forehead.

"I'm so glad you're all right." She had one of those mushy looks on her face. And her voice was as sweet and oozy as maple syrup.

"Dad," Tom said tapping his father's leg. "How did you find me? How did you know?"

"We got to worrying about you and Grampa being home alone," he answered. "So me and your mother came home. Must have got there right after you left. Couldn't have missed you more than a few minutes. Grampa told us where you were headed. So, after we got him loaded in the pickup for Mama to take him to the hospital, I told her to stop at Justin's and have him and his dad come through the shortcut you'd mentioned to Grampa, while I looked for you from this direction.

"Justin's dad had spotted the panther early this morning, prowling around their calf pen. A bunch of the farmers and ranchers were over there. They were hunting the far side of Panther Peak when the blizzard hit, and were back warming up in the house when your mama got there.

"Justin led them right through the shortcut, but if Leonard Hall hadn't heard your shotgun go off, we still might never have found you. He must have heard the shot that killed the panther."

Susan leaned over. "Tell us about it, Tom. Tell us what happened."

"Yeah," Dad said. "How did you do it? All by yourself. Why did you wait till he was right on you? What happened?"

"Why didn't you run?" Mama asked. "How did you kill the panther?"

There were a lot of things Tom could have told them—things that would make their hair stand on end. Only that didn't seem too important now. What was important was knowing that Grampa was all right, that Ginger and her new filly were doing fine, and that the darned, pesky panther was dead.

So all Tom said was, "I sure am tired. You mind if I sleep a little?"

About the Author

BILL WALLACE, author of the award-winning Archway Paperbacks *A Dog Called Kitty* and *Trapped in Death Cave,* is the principal and physical education teacher at West Elementary School in Chickasha, Oklahoma, the same school he attended as a child. A former fourth-grade teacher, Mr. Wallace couldn't find good adventure stories to read to his students that would hold their attention, so he decided to try to write some himself. *Danger on Panther Peak* (originally titled *Shadow on the Snow*), like his previous titles, was also written for his students. Currently, Mr. Wallace lives on a farm outside Chickasha, Oklahoma, with his wife, three daughters, and four horses. On vacations, they swim and explore in the Wichita Mountains, the setting for this novel.